Anthology of Futures

David Reynolds-Moreton

sci-fi-cafe.com

Anthology of Futures
David Reynolds-Moreton

This edition Copyright © 2022 by Oxford eBooks Ltd.
Published under the sci-fi-cafe.com imprint.
www.oxford-ebooks.com
Story Copyright © 1998 by David Reynolds-Moreton

The right of the author to be identified as the author of this work
has been asserted in accordance with the
Copyright, Designs and Patents Act 1988.

All characters and events in this book are fictitious.
Any resemblance to any person living or dead is purely coincidental.

All rights reserved.
No part of this publication may be reproduced, stored in a retrieval system, or
transmitted, in any form or by any means, electronic, mechanical, photocopying,
recording or otherwise, without the prior permission of the copyright owners.

ISBN 978-1-910779-92-7 (Paperback)

sci-fi-cafe.com

Seven stories which foretell the possible futures of Earth

THE CHILL
ENHANCEMENT
BLACKNESS
BRIGHTLIGHT
THE FACTORY
TIME TRIP
TRANSFER UNIT

THE CHILL

IN THE EARLY hours of the morning, several hundred tonnes of ice broke away from the over-hanging lip of the glacier, fell a hundred metres or so to the ground below and smashed into a multitude of fragments.

The ground shook, as did Gleeson's little wooden hut, rattling his few possessions and awakening him with a start from a long and peaceful sleep.

He looked around the interior of his refuge, and as nothing had actually fallen down and the walls were still standing, he pulled the fur coverings of his bed over his head, shutting out the bitter cold of the night.

Two yellow-green eyes in the far corner of his hut reflected the faint light from the dying embers of the fire, growing larger as the wolf pad padded across the wooden floor of the hut, and thrust a cold wet nose under the furs of Gleeson's bed, seeking out his face. Having found it, the nose tucked itself under his chin, gave a little grunt of greeting, and withdrew.

'It's alright Wolf, we'll see what happened in the morning.'

Wolf gave another grunt and padded back to his pile of furs, turned around twice, and curled up to sleep the rest of the darkness away.

Night and morning were separated by a small difference of light levels at this time of the year, as the snowfall was almost continuous in its relentless attempt to cover the world in a deep mantle of white. Soon both man and wolf were deep in their sleep cycle, their bodies recovering from the exertions of the previous day.

Some two years previously, Gleeson had been hacking apart a dead hollow tree stump for firewood, when he noticed a tiny bundle of fur tucked away in one corner.

He froze, and then slowly stepped back a few paces, his hunting knife held at the ready.

He looked around for paw prints. There were none, not even the little snow filled hollows which would have been left if the she wolf had left the area several hours ago. She must have abandoned her last remaining cub through lack of food, or maybe she had succumbed to the intense cold while out hunting.

Gleeson reached into the recess of the stump and picked up the little cub. It was painfully thin and seemed to be dead, and then two tiny eyes opened and looked straight into his, while a very faint trembling could be felt through his thick gloves.

Should he leave it, letting nature take its natural course, or should he... a faint whimper reached his fur covered ears, and the decision was made for him. Tucking the tiny creature into the top of his jacket, he gathered up the wood he had cut, loaded it onto the sledge and set off for his hut.

With the wood he had collected safely stacked in the covered wood stack, Gleeson went to his larder, a hole in the permafrost with a heavy wooden trap door, and withdrew two pieces of hard frozen meat.

Placing one piece in his cooking pot along with some snow, he stoked up the fire and put the pot on to boil. He placed some furs on wolf cub in front of the now roaring fire, its tiny flanks hardly moving as it hung on to life.

When the meat had been cooked, he set it aside, replenished his stock of firewood and waited for the broth to cool.

Cradling the little cub in one hand, Gleeson tried to dribble the now lukewarm liquid into the cub's mouth, forcing it open with one finger.

After the first few drops of meat juice had entered its mouth, it greedily drank the rest, and then Gleeson ground up the remaining meat into a thin paste.

That too was gulped down. He knew it wasn't the cub's natural food, but it was all he had to offer. Putting the cub down on the furs, he then set about getting his own meal, consisting of roasted bear meat and a large cup of pine needle tea.

As the days went by, the cub grew and put on weight with Gleeson's tender care. He was glad of the company, for he had been on his own since his parents had been killed in an ice fall many years ago, and he hadn't seen a human being since.

The pair became inseparable, but knowing it was a wild animal, Gleeson never forgot that when full grown it could turn on him, once the wolf's true nature came into play. Or so he thought, until one day, he was confronted by the biggest black bear he had ever seen.

The bear came out of nowhere, throwing up the powdery snow as it charged towards its intended meal. Gleeson was trapped, behind him was a thicket of tangled scrub, long dead but impenetrable, while to each side the snow had drifted into three-metre-high banks. His hunting knife and a long stave were no match for the charging bear, and Gleeson thought this time he would die.

A grey streak flashed past him, with a blood-curdling howl from bared fangs, as Wolf launched itself at the bear. Somehow it twisted in mid air, landing on the bear's back and sank its teeth deep into the black neck. The bear reared upright, and let out a roar which shook the snow from the nearby trees.

Again, the fangs sank deeply into the bear's neck, drawing copious amounts of blood. The bear dropped to all fours to shake off its attacker, but Wolf was one step ahead, and had already dropped to the ground to go for the underbelly, ripping out a huge piece of flesh.

It was too much for the bear, who turned and fled with Wolf in pursuit, nipping at the retreating flanks and drawing even more blood.

Gleeson sank to the ground, trembling, as the bear and Wolf disappeared down the slope in a flurry of fine powdered snow, the roars from the bear fading into the distance.

After what seemed like an eternity, Wolf returned and gave Gleeson's cheek a lick in greeting before cleaning the bear's blood from its fur. He now knew that he could trust Wolf, as in nature, a lone wolf would never tackle a fully grown black bear.

Gleeson had had enough for one day, and decided to return to his hut, but Wolf, who had trotted off in the direction of the fleeing bear, had stopped, turned and given a short yelp before going out of sight down the slope. Gleeson, not wishing to be left alone, followed to find Wolf standing a few metres away from the stricken bear, lying prone and breathing shallowly in the blood stained snow.

He picked up a fallen branch, and advancing slowly, threw it, hitting the bear squarely on the head. The bear didn't seem to notice this affront to its person, and just lay there, its life blood slowly seeping away.

Wolf slowly crept forward to within a metre of the bear, looked at Gleeson, and gave another short yelp. He realised that Wolf was trying to tell him something, but what was it? Maybe that it was safe to put the bear out of its misery? He thought so.

Gleeson drew his hunting knife, and approaching the bear from behind, plunged the blade deep into the upper neck, severing the brain stem. The huge bear gave a final shudder, and then lay still.

A fine pelt and a huge quantity of fresh meat was too much to pass up, and Gleeson set to the grisly job of butchery.

With the skin on the sledge, fur side down, Gleeson piled on the best cuts of bear meat until he wondered if he would be able to haul it back to the hut. Meanwhile, Wolf tucked into the biggest feast he had had in many months. That which Gleeson couldn't carry, he left for the other animals of the nearby forest, knowing it would not remain there for long.

Apart from the occasional black bear, elk, and rarely seen wolf, there was little life left in the area in which he lived. Most other wildlife had fled south from the ever-advancing ice wall of the glacier.

He remembered his parents telling him of warmer times, when bushes grew sweet berries and plants which could be eaten grew on the ground, but he didn't remember them. Perhaps they were before the time of his parents too, and they only told him of that which they had been told.

Although the warm days of which his parents had spoken were very short, they did at least allow the growth of something called grass and moss, on which herds of deer, rabbits and other creatures fed, but those days were long gone too, and he couldn't remember them either.

His main fear was the ice. It seemed to advance more quickly each day, and several times he had seen it actually move. Gleeson's hut was only a kilometre or so from the ever-advancing glacier, and he would have to move his hut again soon. But there was nowhere to go, as the next thing south was a cliff and then the frozen sea. His father had said that the sea was once a liquid, with waves crashing on the shore below the cliffs. But that was only hearsay, he had never seen it.

Gleeson just made it back to his hut before exhaustion set in, and his legs gave way under the strain. Somehow, he would have to get his haul of meat into the cold store.

He managed to find the energy to store the meat, and then, exhausted, went into his hut for a well-earned rest, and a reappraisal of his relationship with Wolf.

As far as he was concerned, his world had always been one of snow, the glacier, and the shortage of food. He had never known anything else, even when his parents were alive. In his lifetime, he had noticed the wildlife was getting scarcer as their food source depleted. He reasoned that most animals had somehow got down the cliff and across the frozen sea to some other land, that's if one existed. His parents said it did, but they had never been there that he could recall.

Somewhere in the dim memory of his childhood, he seemed to remember water in the warmer days of the summer, little pools here and there, icicles melting in the weak sunlight, but he had never seen the sea, so he didn't know if it was frozen or not. He knew one day he would have to cross it, as the glacier was advancing at an ever-increasing rate, and he was running out of land.

The cliff was about a kilometre away, and once he had gone there just to see what it was like. A sheer drop of ten metres down to a gentle slope and then a flat whiteness which went out to the far horizon. So where was the other land? He hadn't seen any, and doubted its existence. But one day he would have to get down there and travel across it, if he was not to be crushed by the glacier.

Accepting the inevitable, Gleeson had begun to collect suitable timber to build a much bigger sledge, as he realised the one he used to collect his firewood was not big enough to carry his food stocks, tools, firewood and the portable stove to melt snow for drinking and cooking. In the back of his mind there grew an idea of a sail to propel the sledge, as it would be far too heavy to pull with all his possessions on board.

A small collection of woodworking tools, passed down through the generations enabled him to construct his modular hut, which had to be moved piece by piece as the glacier advanced. A collection of furs which hung on the internal walls helped to keep the bitter cold out, and the fireplace he had built from stones laboriously dug out of the permafrost provided a little warmth and the means to cook his meat.

Gleeson was reluctant to leave his hut and the meagre comforts it provided, but he had no option, as the glacier was getting nearer and would push him off the cliff in time, also the food supply was dwindling.

But it had not always been like this, according to his parents. They told of days when the winter was cold with plenty of snow, and the summers were warm, and one could go about with very little clothing on. There were fruit trees, berries and something called vegetables, which could be grown, dug up, and eaten. How long ago this was, he had no idea, it certainly wasn't in his lifetime, or even that of his parents.

According to the old legends, which had been passed down from generation to generation, and probably altered, there had been a catastrophic change in the climate, brought about by a vast outpouring of light from the sun. Many people died from the burning rays, and great fires burnt the world's forests, killing huge amounts of wildlife.

Only those in cooler climes, or who were able to seek shelter, survived. This was followed by a series of volcanic eruptions, which for a time shielded the planet with copious amounts of dust, cooling the world down and making day and night almost the same. When the dust storms cleared, the sun had dimmed its output of light considerably, and the great cold began. Worryingly, it seemed to get colder with the passage of time, as the glaciers advanced southwards.

Gradually the fruit bearing trees, those with broad leaves and the bushes which bore berries, died out, unable to withstand the advancing cold. Grasses lasted a little longer, but they too succumbed in the end, leaving the pines and a form of moss and lichen for the small herds of hardy deer and elk to live on. Unfortunately, the carnivores lived off these, along with the few remaining humans. In time, only the carnivores remained, feeding off each other until they too became scarce.

The advancing glacier had forced what life remained southwards, the great cliffs and the sea forming the southern barrier. This sustained the few remaining humans for a time, but one by one they too perished, or were eaten in an unguarded moment.

Even as a child, he could not remember anyone else apart from his parents, and now they too were no more. Loneliness was something he had got used to, but the arrival of the wolf cub, now full grown, reminded him of what it was really like to be on one's own, and he was grateful for the wolf's company.

His parents had told him more of how the earth had been before the catastrophe - a very hot zone way down south, consisting of hot sand and rocks. He wondered if it still existed, or it too had been covered in snow.

Once or twice in his lifetime the snowfall had stopped, and a pale round light appeared high up in the blue sky, but it didn't last for long, and the snow once more blanked out everything.

Perhaps one day everything would get back to normal, whatever normal was, but he didn't put much hope on it.

Generally, he was kept busy just surviving, and that was getting tougher by the day, as the animals he depended on for food became harder to find and kill.

A series of deep rumbles and a cooking pot falling to the floor awoke Gleeson and Wolf for the second time that night, or to be more exact, that morning, although it was only slightly lighter than the last time.

Rubbing the sleep from his eyes, Gleeson staggered over to the fire, put some more logs onto the few remaining embers and fanned the fire into life. The two pieces of meat he had taken from the cold store last night had thawed a little, and he placed his piece onto the stone slab to roast while Wolf's piece of shin was laid just below to finish thawing. He often wondered why Wolf had never helped himself to the meat during the night, but he never had, always waiting for his master to give it to him.

A welcoming hot brew of pine needle tea and a chunk of roast bear meat set Gleeson up for the day, while Wolf hungrily chewed away at his tougher portion of meat. A quick tidy up of the hut, and they were ready for what the new day might hold for them.

Armed with his hunting knife, metal tipped stave and the crossbow, the pair set off, side by side, for the glacier.

Gleeson was worried about the increasing speed with which the ice was advancing, and wondered if he still had time to finish the big sledge which would hopefully take them across the frozen sea to a place of safety. He hadn't quite solved the problem of the sail, thinking perhaps it could be made from thinned animal hides, stitched together with sinews.

The marker sticks he had placed in a row, to measure the glacier's forward advance, had all been overrun and were buried under the huge mound of snow the glacier had thrust before it. At this rate of advancement, he would have to speed up the building of the sledge.

The ground under Gleeson's feet trembled, and there was a deep rumbling sound as the glacier moved forward another ten centimetres, pushing the huge pile of snow before it.

A group of pine trees further along the glacier's front suddenly waved to and fro, and then fell, unable to withstand the mighty forces against them. A startled elk which had been sheltering in the trees disentangled itself from the flaying branches, and before Gleeson could bring his crossbow to bear, it had disappeared into the curtain of falling snow. He was sorry he had missed the opportunity of another skin to add to his collection, as he needed all he could get to make the sail for the big sledge.

A few faint footprints in the snow suggested that an arctic hare had not long passed this way. Gleeson had not tasted hare for a long time, and he followed the tracks until they disappeared on the edge of a large ice sheet. Wolf sniffed at the last visible foot-print and then snuffled his way across the ice, to pick up the tracks some fifty metres further on.

Something in the distance moved, white on white, but the movement gave its position away. The crossbow was loaded with a bolt and brought to Gleeson's shoulder in one swift movement. The bolt sang in the icy air as it sped towards its target. The hare, seeing something move, ducked down, but it was too late. The bolt, with its bright blue flight feathers, pinned the hare to the hardened snow behind it. If it had not been for the coloured feathers, Gleeson would never have seen it against the glaring white of the surrounding snow.

With the bolt safely back in its quiver, and the hare slung from Gleeson's belt, he headed off towards the remains of what had once been a mighty forest of pines. Wolf gave the still steaming entrails of the hare a disdainful sniff, and then followed his master.

Most of the trees had died from the continuous intense cold, but from the few which had survived, Gleeson gathered some of the choicest pine needles to make his 'pine tea', thus, unknowingly, supplying his body's vitamin C requirement.

The construction of the big sledge would strain every bit of Gleeson's abilities and his rather meagre store of materials. There was still plenty of dead wood to collect and be split into strips, but he realised that metal blades set into the runners were a must, if the sledge was to be steered on the ice of the frozen sea.

He entered the cabin, and after putting away his hunting gear, went over to the wooden box which contained what few tools and metal scraps that had been collected over the ages. Now there was nothing to find, all signs of civilisation having long ceased to exist in his part of the world.

The box held a few files, a saw, a hammer, and some drill bits, along with several strips of metal which he would need for the sledge runners. An assortment of other bits, rods, a few nails and a coil of wire were all that were left of a mechanised age of affluence, ground out of existence by the ever-encroaching ice field, the bitter cold, and the smothering snow.

Gleeson selected four strips of metal of about equal size, and with an almost blunt file, rounded one end of each piece such that it would not catch on any protruding pieces of ice when inserted in the sledge runners. The construction of the sledge took longer than he expected, as each piece of the frame had to be split from a dead log, trimmed to shape and then bound together with rawhide. As it was so cold outside, the assembly had to take place inside his hut, which left very little room to move around, causing many a bruise and a shortened temper. Wolf looked on in bewilderment, as this was far removed from hunting, eating and sleeping.

The sail slowly took shape, the hides of whatever he could catch, plus his wall coverings being scraped as thin as he could get them while still retaining enough strength to hold the wind.

After several more ground shaking lumps of ice had fallen from the ever-advancing ice sheet, Gleeson wondered if he would finish his sledge in time.

The metal blades were set in the main sledge runners by heating a thinner piece of metal until it was red hot, and then burning a deep groove in the runner. This was then scraped out to remove the burnt wood, and the blade set in the groove so formed with heated resin from the pine trees.

Once cooled, the blades seemed to be firmly locked into the runners, much to Gleeson's satisfaction. The mast would be held upright with rawhide strips, several being braided together to give them the extra strength they would need in a high wind.

Once the main body of the sledge had been completed, he set about building compartments to take his stock of frozen meat, the toolbox and the portable stove, along with a good supply of wood.

A double thickness sleeping bag was constructed, with enough room for wolf as well, although he didn't know if wolf would get in it, as he seemed to prefer to sleep on his own.

Only one thing remained to be done, and that was to find a way down to the frozen sea without a sheer drop of several metres to the beach below. Gleeson hadn't explored much of the coastline, as there had been no need to, but he would have to now.

Before setting off for the sea, Gleeson tried to move the sledge and found it very difficult, not only because of the confined space, but because of the weight. He wondered if wolf would take kindly to a simple harness to help him to pull it, and so he made one with the left-over rawhide.

Carrying the crossbow and his hunting knife, the pair set off for the cliffs, wolf racing on ahead looking for something to chase, but there was no sign of anything living, the intense cold having killed it, or driven it south across the sea.

The wind had dropped a little and the snowfall was reduced to a few vagrant flakes giving a clear view out to the horizon. It was just a great expanse of whiteness and quite flat, except for where something had forced the ice upwards into huge and menacing mounds, and the driving snow had added to it.

The pair trudged along the cliff edge for some distance before the land dipped down to what had once been a beach. It would mean a lot of hard work to get the sledge this far on soft snow, but worth it, as the sea seemed to be quite flat and free of snow as far as Gleeson could tell. He assumed that the wind had driven it onto the land, as the wind seemed to come in from the south across the frozen sea.

He was about to turn back towards his hut when he noticed a huge fountain of what looked like free water shoot skyward, pause, and then drop back down to the frozen sea. Seconds later, a loud crack followed by a massive roar sounded, as the water spout reached the land. Perhaps it was gushes of water like that which explained why the frozen sea was so flat, as in time the flow of free water would smooth out the unevenness caused by the sea freezing in the first place.

On their way back to the hut, Gleeson realised he would need some way of steering the sledge, as the metal blades he had set in the runners would hold it on a straight course. The best he could come up with was another blade set in the end of a pole set at the back of the sledge, which could be pushed to one side and pressed down onto the ice.

That night, the ever-advancing wall of ice shed another massive piece of its upper lip with a tremendous roar, and with the weight on the leading edge now relieved, the ice wall advanced another few metres towards Gleeson's hut, as the stresses evened out. The towering mass of the glacier was now visible from Gleeson's hut, as he found out next morning.

He would have to dismantle the end wall of his hut in order to drag the sledge outside and then stock it with his provisions, as it would be too heavy to move across the non-slippery wooden floor of the hut if fully laden.

Another earth-shaking rumble from the glacier indicated it was on the move again, and he began to panic, in case he couldn't get the sledge out before the glacier swept it and his hut over the cliff and onto the frozen beach below.

Wolf looked on in bewilderment as Gleeson began ripping out the end of the hut, hoping the roof wouldn't collapse on him in the process. A creak and a squeal announced that another chunk of ice was about to descend earthwards, and then with an ear-splitting crash it did so, showering the pair in small shards of ice. With the last of the end wall dismantled, Gleeson began levering the sledge out into the open, wondering how he would be able to drag it down to the cliff and along to where it sloped to the beach below.

With the provisions stored in their boxes and the wooden chest with all his tools and materials safely aboard, Gleeson slipped into the pulling harness, but failed to move the sledge more than a few centimetres. Desperation swept over him, as he realised he had destroyed his hut and was now stuck with an immoveable sledge, and with a rumble, the ice was on the move again.

He looked around for the small harness he had made for wolf, and seeing it hanging from a peg on the now sagging wall of his hut, grabbed it, and called wolf over to him.

Wolf stood still while he slipped the loop of the harness around wolf's neck and then put his own harness on. With a desperate cry of 'Come on wolf' Gleeson put all his weight on the harness, and the sledge moved forward. Within seconds, wolf had grasped the idea, and panting hard, put his not inconsiderable pulling power into his harness and they were moving, heading for the sea cliffs and away from the threat of being overwhelmed by the glacier.

By the time the pair had reached the cliffs, Gleeson's legs ached and wolf's heaving flanks told of the effort he had put in to moving the heavily laden sledge. He bent down and patted wolf's head in gratitude, all wolf could manage was a short grunt between rasping breaths. They had made it, gaining fifty or so metres on the advancing ice. Where the snow had compacted, the sledge moved quite easily, foretelling how it would likely slide freely once it was on the sea ice.

After a much-needed rest, the pair continued along the cliff edge, zig-zagging from frozen patch of snow to the next, as soft snow threatened to bring the sledge to a standstill. At long last, the decline down to the beach came into view and the sledge picked up speed, Gleeson and wolf having to increase speed considerably, so as not to be over run.

At last, they were at the edge of the frozen sea, and after a bit of a struggle getting over the soft foam-like edge where it joined the beach, they were onto solid ice.

Suddenly, a great spout of water gushed up into the air, some five hundred metres ahead of them, and then fell back to spill across the ice, filling up all the small holes and gaps caused by the buckling of the ice as it had frozen.

Gleeson looked back once more at the world he had known for so long, most of it now obscured by the towering wall of moving ice, which had swept all before it.

The sun was only visible as a pale light in the sky ahead, and Gleeson, knowing he had to head south, thought if he took his bearings from the sun at its highest point in the sky each day, it should guide them on their way.

With a final heave, Gleeson had the sledge pointing what he thought was south, and began to haul up the sail; Wolf, sensing that something different was about to happen, jumped up besides his master and lay down on the only bit of free deck space left. With the sail only half up, the sledge began to move, quickly gathering speed as the sail reached the top of the mast and the haul-up rope was made fast.

Looking back after a few minutes, he was surprised to see how far they had gone. The cliff was just a smudge on the horizon, with the massive glacier above it and not looking so menacing now. Wolf gave a little grunt, dropped his head onto his paws, and went to sleep.

The frozen sea was surprisingly smooth, with only the occasional large lump of ice protruding from its surface, and Gleeson easily steered the sledge around such obstacles; the steel blades almost sang on the ice as the wind picked up, and he dropped the sail just a little, as he was still getting used to the idea of sailing a large lump of wood across an ice field.

He thought about why the sea was so smooth and flat, and he remembered the water spout he had seen earlier. As the ice grew thicker, it expanded, putting pressure on the water below and trapped air pockets acted like small pressure vessels. When the pressure was too much, the ice buckled and cracked, the trapped air then pushed the water out of the fracture until the pressure was relieved. The water then spilled out over the frozen sea, evening out any irregularities and leaving a reasonably smooth surface.

Gleeson had no sense of actual time, only day and night, and sometimes during the year, even that was hard to differentiate. When he thought it was about nightfall because of the dimming light, he dropped the sail and guided the sledge into the leeward side of a large ice block, driving one of his precious metal rods into the block and tying the sledge to it, so that it would not get blown away during the night should the wind increase.

By now they were both hungry, and Gleeson placed the flat slate like stone he had brought along on the deck, and erected his homemade wood burner. With a pot of ice chips melting on the fire, the smell of boiling bear meat soon pervaded the chill evening air, and Wolf awoke to sit upright next to the fire, a thin dribble of saliva falling from his jaws in anticipation.

They had to wait awhile for the pot to cool down, and then the meat was shared out between them, Wolf gulping his portion down with hardly a chew, as do most canines. The meat juice was also split between them, nothing was going to be wasted. By now it had got darker, the wind had died down, and Gleeson got out his home-made sleeping bag and crawled in, Wolf snuggling up to him, more for security than warmth.

Several days of speeding across the ice brought a change in the amount of snowfall, it seemed much less now with smaller flakes, and brief glimpses of the sun made locating the southerly direction he wanted much easier.

Gleeson had stopped for the mid day break, and Wolf had bounded off across the ice for the sheer joy of moving after having to lie still for so long. A series of sharp barks, which he had not heard Wolf make before, attracted his attention. A dark shape, just a little bigger than Wolf, was being held at bay by a snarling Wolf. The creature, (a seal) the like of which Gleeson had never seen before, was trying to get back to a hole in the ice made by a water gusher, but Wolf was barring its way.

Gleeson grabbed his crossbow and advanced slowly, not knowing if the animal was dangerous or just a potential source of food. Wolf was darting from side to side, keeping the seal from escaping into its more usual watery domain, with bared teeth and the occasional snarl. Gleeson took careful aim, the crossbow sang its message of death, and the seal slumped to the ice with a bolt through its head. Wolf moved in and gave the seal a sniff, looked up at his master and gave a little yelp. They were a very good team.

The seal was skinned, the flesh stripped from the carcass and stored on the sledge, and Wolf enjoyed his reward. Gleeson went over to the hole in the frozen sea and was surprised to see the ice was not much more that a metre thick, the water rising and falling rhythmically within the hole. Gleeson reasoned out that there must be a large area of free water for the movement in the hole to exist. He recalled his parents telling him of how the sea used to be, with waves crashing on the shore and the tide going in and out - but that was a long time ago, and before his parent's time - it was an old story, and maybe had been added to over the years.

He decided to check the next hole they came across to see if the ice was really getting thinner, as this would be a threat to their survival if they didn't make landfall before the ice ran out.

Gleeson set the sledge for due south when the sun was at its highest point, and they were on their way again. Several days later, and the snow had ceased to fall. The sun was now a bright ball of fire in the sky, with a few fluffy clouds against the blue background.

The next water hole they came across nearly spelt the end of their journey, Gleeson spotting it just in time to steer the sledge to one side in a flurry of ice chips. Upon inspection, the ice was now only half a metre thick, and the water in the hole was rising and falling with much more force. He wondered if this was getting near the end of their frozen world - and what they would find when they got there?

As they continued south, they came across more and more piles of fractured ice, having to steer carefully between them, and on one occasion they had to hack a passageway where two massive walls of ice almost met, to get to the other side.

On the horizon Gleeson could see a long dark smudge, with a column of smoke rising up into the clear blue sky. Was this the land they had hoped to reach? His parents had made no mention of a smoking hill.

The wind had dropped to almost a whisper now, and every now and again the sledge needed a little push to get it going again, which was just as well, as a loud crack heralded the parting of the ice they were on from the main sheet behind. There was little they could do except wait to see what would happen next. Slowly, the ice sheet moved in a southerly direction, leaving clear water behind them, so Gleeson pushed the sledge into what he thought would be the middle of his floating island.

Ocean currents moved the ice sheet towards the land mass, but the movement of the waves was causing the sheet to break up, and Wolf was getting restless. Gleeson had to reposition the sledge several times, trying to keep it on the biggest piece of ice, and wondering just what to do if the ice sank when it got too small to bear the weight of the sledge.

As they drifted on, the land began to take shape; he could just make out what looked like a sandy beach with trees stretching up into the hills. Beyond this, he couldn't see much detail, as the whole area above the trees seemed to be hidden in a thin mist or haze.

As they neared the beach, the ocean swell increased, and more bits of the ice sheet broke off. And then a particularly large swell lifted the ice sheet up, and they were surfing towards the beach. When the ice hit the beach, Gleeson leapt from the front of the sledge and onto the sand, hauling it off the ice with the towing harness which was still attached. He managed to get the whole contraption clear of the water, and lay down on the soft sand, exhausted. Wolf came up to him, gave his face a lick and then lay down beside him. They had made it - but where were they? It was nothing like the lands he had been told about.

After a long rest, Gleeson removed all his precious tools, the wood burner and anything else he thought might be needed up to the top of the beach, well away from the highest tide. The meat stocks were nearly exhausted and in a state of thaw, so a quick meal was prepared and gulped down by both of them.

The air felt quite warm, and scented, compared to what they had been used to on the ice sheet up North, and Gleeson wondered how he could preserve any meat for future use - that's if he could find any in the first place. Just above the beach was a little clearing in the trees, covered in what he assumed must be grass. It was soft, green, and looked like what his parents had described.

As it was getting a little dark, and their appetites had been satisfied by gorging on the remains of their stored bear meat, Gleeson set up a campfire from the ample supply of dead wood on the shore line, and settled down for a well earned sleep, Wolf curling up besides him as always.

They were both awakened next morning by a series of squawks, tweets, and other sounds as the dawn chorus got under way. Both were hungry and thirsty, but all they had was a small supply of dried bear meat, and nothing to drink.

Gleeson somehow knew the sea water was not suitable for drinking, but he went down to the sea just to be sure. There was no sign of the ice sheet they had arrived on, nor was there any ice in sight - just rolling waves right out to the horizon. He wet his hand in the sea, tasted it, and knew his first thoughts on the matter were correct - Wolf just gave it a sniff, and retreated. Gleeson knew they had to find drinkable water, and soon. Armed with his crossbow, hunting knife and spear, the pair set off along the beach, not knowing quite why, but it seemed to be the right thing to do. A mere three hundred metres along the shoreline, and they came across a small stream, tumbling down from a rocky outcrop. Wolf was first to reach the water and drink, quickly followed by Gleeson, who first washed his grubby hands, and then drank deeply. The water tasted sweet compared to the melted ice and snow he was used to, and he wondered why.

The clearing in the forest seemed to be a good place to make a permanent camp, but first they had to find a source of meat. Back at the clearing, Gleeson removed his furs as he was getting too hot, and they struck inland to look for food, breaking twigs along the way to mark their passage. A grunting noise stopped them both in their tracks - some way ahead a grey, brown shape was rooting about in the bushes, but as they quietly approached, it sensed their presence and moved away.

Wolf gave a soft grunt and trotted off to one side, slowly working his way around their quarry, so forcing it towards Gleeson, who stood rock still with the crossbow at the ready. The bolt flew straight and true, and the wild boar slumped to the ground. In Gleeson's book, if it moved, it could be eaten - so the boar was quartered up and carried back to the clearing. Wolf ate his share raw, but Gleeson preferred cooked meat, so the fire was lit in the wood burner, the pot half filled with water from the stream and put on, and soon the smell of boiled pork wafted through the woodland glade. He wondered if the smell would attract other animals - but none came. The rest of the meat was cut into strips and dried over the fire, as there was no way he could freeze it.

It took many days for Gleeson to construct his hut, cutting down trees, splitting them into crude planks, and using wooden pegs to hold the whole thing together. A stone chimney was constructed in one corner to take away the smoke from the wood burner, but it would be a while before he made a table and chair like the ones he had in his old hut, back on the ice.

One day, while sitting on a rock which protruded out into the sea, he noticed his first fish. It moved - so it could be eaten, if he could catch it. Careful observation revealed the fact that large fish ate smaller ones - so if he could make a hook and attach a smaller one to it…

Rummaging about in his box of treasures, he found some hard wire, and from this he fashioned a hook, attaching a long thin piece of sinew to it, he now had the basic means of fishing.

Wolf didn't like fish, but Gleeson found it very palatable, and often sat on his rock, line a dangling.

Once the hut was finished to Gleeson's satisfaction, and a reliable food source established, he turned his attention to exploring this strange land. The pair had made many journeys deep into the forest, but it seemed to be just more of the same in all directions. On one trip, Gleeson had climbed a tall tree, leaving a worried looking Wolf on the ground, and found he could see the distant smoking hill he had seen from the ice floe. Wolf was overjoyed upon his return to terra firma, and insisted on standing on his hind legs to lick Gleeson's face repeatedly.

The day came when Gleeson decided to try and find the smoking hill; armed as usual, they set out for the tall tree he had climbed earlier, and from that set the direction for their goal, marking the way as they went along. The ground began to rise, several small streams were crossed, and at last the forest ended in a sloping plain of rough gravel and sand, which led up to the volcano.

It was the size of it that amazed Gleeson, the cone towered up into the sky, and a deep throated roar accompanied the huge column of white smoke, as it raced up into the atmosphere. There was something odd about the smoke, but he didn't understand what it was. As far as he could recall, smoke was whitish, sometimes tinged with blue and on occasions a little black, depending on what he was burning - but this was a pure white, almost brilliant. The seething column must have been several kilometres across, although it was difficult to judge, as there was nothing else around to compare it against.

Suddenly Wolf stopped; he raised a paw and put it down several times before backing towards Gleeson, who was several metres behind him. Something was amiss, and Gleeson, knowing that Wolf often sensed things he had missed, went forward and bent down to touch the ground. It was warm, and a few metres further on it was positively hot. This was something Gleeson had never experienced before - hot ground. There seemed little point in going further on up the slope, as the surface just got hotter, so they circled around, keeping to what Gleeson thought of as normal ground.

Unknown to Gleeson, a very long time ago, tectonic plate movement had caused a rent to form on the ocean bed. It ran along just under the surface and then down to terminate in the top of an active magma chamber. Huge amounts of sea water poured into the vent and down to the top of the white-hot chamber - instantly turning to high pressure steam. The massive weight of the ocean above prevented the water backing up, so the steam pressure just built up until it could be restrained no more, found the old lava exit, and just blew the top of the volcano cap off; the super-heated steam vented upwards to condense into white water vapour along with massive amounts of volcanic ash, as it streamed high into the atmosphere, as the old volcano cleared it's throat.

The clouds of ash and water vapour so produced travelled around the world, reflecting the suns heat from reaching Earth's surface, and so the big chill began. What compounded the disaster was the magma itself. Normally, with that much cooling from the sea water, the magma would eventually chill and set, blocking off the water flow; but this chamber was a little different - the magma, as it cooled, increased in density and flowed back down the sides of the chamber to be reheated from below, and return to the top in a never-ending cycle.

In time, but a very long time, the magma chamber would cool enough for the cycle to be broken - and this was happening now. In the early days, the water vapour would not have been seen until it had reached the upper atmosphere, such was the heat of the steam; now Gleeson was seeing the end of the cycle, as he saw actual white-water vapour leaving the vent.

The pair had travelled a good way around the volcano when Gleeson noticed fine water droplets falling from above, on the leeward side of the smoking monster. He had never seen rain, only snow, and it was a while before he put two and two together to come up with what was really happening.

They returned to their hut in the clearing, Wolf happy to be home, and Gleeson with a head full of ideas whirling around, as he tried to explain to himself what had happened to his world.

By now, Gleeson, recalling what his parents had said about fruit and berries so long ago, had tried most of those he had found. Some made him sick, while others were very palatable and were added to his diet. Wolf didn't do fruit and berries - if it wasn't red, and at some stage had been moving, he just ignored it.

The pair had been well settled in their hut for a couple of months when Gleeson got to thinking what else might lie undiscovered in his new land, as the fairly short excursions they had made so far only revealed more of the same. They set off along the shoreline to see what they could find. For some time, he had realised that they could live off the land quite well as they travelled around, so little in supplies were carried on these expeditions.

The occasional rocky outcrop, which went out for some distance into the sea, forced them to climb up the cliffs and onto higher ground. It was on one of these occasions that Gleeson got a view up through a long valley of the smoking hill, as he liked to think of it, and found it wasn't smoking very much at all. Just a few wisps of water vapour, lazily drifting up into the clear blue sky - and no roar. The magma chamber had sealed at last.

For several days now, there had been almost clear blue skies, with just a few fluffy white clouds drifting around - and it was getting hotter. Neither of them were used to such heat, and Gleeson shed almost all his clothes, while Wolf panted a lot, and then shed his thick coat, rubbing against any rock or tree he could find to rid himself of his winter fur.

They had been travelling for nearly two months along the shoreline and up the deep valleys, discovering many new things and foods, and then one day Wolf gave an excited yelp and bounded up the beach to disappear into the tree line. Gleeson followed to find Wolf standing outside their hut, his tail furiously swinging to and fro and his lips peeled back in a grin. They were home again.

Slowly, over time, the vast clouds of water vapour condensed into rain, taking the volcanic dust with them and the normal seasons were restored. Gleeson and Wolf were getting older, and then one day Wolf didn't get up to greet his master in the morning with the usual wet lick and yelp. He buried Wolf near the hut, somehow feeling that if he did so, he would be able to feel the presence of his old friend.

Many days later, Gleeson saw a large sailing boat heading into the little bay opposite his hut, but not knowing what it was, stayed out of sight in the scrub which lined the beach to see what would happen. A rowing boat with several people in it came ashore, and then he realised they must have seen the smoke from his fire and had come to see who was here. They called out in a tongue he didn't understand, and then one of them approached the bushes he was hiding behind. In his innocence, Gleeson walked out to greet the man, who, when he saw him, extended a hand and smiled. Soon the others joined the stranger, and a confusing babble of voices left Gleeson wondering if he had done the right thing in showing himself.

Three of the men got back into the boat and rowed out to the ship, returning with another man of paler skin, like Gleeson's, who strode purposefully up the beach towards him. This man spoke in a similar tongue to Gleeson, and he was able to make out most of what was said.

The large sailing boat, along with three others, had been scouring the oceans for any signs of life after the climate had returned to near normal. People were few and far between, and the ships were trying to find as many as they could to build up a viable colony. Gleeson was invited to join them, and decided to do so - without Wolf, the loneliness was beginning to get to him. He paid one last visit to where he had buried Wolf, said good-bye as best he could, collected his precious tools, and joined the group in the rowing boat. There were several who spoke his language, or something very like it, on the big ship, and he soon settled down to this new way of life, although the motion of the ship took a little getting used to.

ENHANCEMENT

BRODRICK CAME OUT of his dream shaking and feeling none too well, and this wasn't the first time he had experienced it. He assumed it was a dream, for there was no other explanation, and yet it had a reality like no dream he'd ever had. He lay there for a while, trying to make sense of the impossible, and failed.

Nearly a year ago he had lost both of his parents in a car crash, and as far as he knew he had no other relations – for all intents and purposes, he was alone.

He now lived in a one room apartment in the less salubrious part of town, as he'd lost the only job he had ever had – the firm went bankrupt. He tried in vain to get another job of like kind, but all he could find was helping out in a fast-food shop, and that just about paid his rent, with a little left over to cover his other necessities.

The dreams had been occurring for several weeks, and each time they became more real – and he didn't like them. He had tried staying up late until he could no longer keep his eyes open, but still they came, not every night, but enough to be disturbing.

The first time it happened, he'd had trouble getting off to sleep. His mind was racing about the situation he was in as he desperately sought a way of bettering his lot in life. All of a sudden there was a wrenching sensation, almost as though he had been pulled out of his body, and he was standing on a barren landscape in a grey light, tendrils of what seemed to be mist swirling about him, and it was bone chillingly cold.

Something off to his right was on the move, a slow, steady slithering sound as the small stones and gravel which made up the landscape gave way to whatever it was.

Somehow he knew it was dangerous and it had sensed his presence. The sounds came closer and his heart thundered in his chest as he urgently sought some means of escape. He could only see a few metres, and that was indistinct, just the odd larger stone among the many smaller ones and gravel which covered the ground.

And then he woke up, trembling from the unseen threat in his dream. Over the next few weeks there were more nights of the same dream, all ending at the same point. And then he was back in it again.

He took a few tentative steps forward and the slithering sound seemed a little less, but it soon gained in volume as the creature slowly headed in his direction.

A few more steps and the ground sloped upwards, a chill wind momentarily blew the mist to the side and he could see a huge cliff ahead. As he took a tentative step toward this change in the landscape, he awoke. The grey light of dawn seeped in through his window, but he could still feel the cold stones under his feet, and then he realised he was safely in his bed – there were no stones or slithering sounds, just the low drum of distant traffic as the city came to life. He didn't like it, but it was only a dream.

Several nights later and that wrenching sensation – and he was back in the grey world of stones, mist and the threatening slithery sound. The slope before him was quite steep, and the stones under his feet give way noisily as he powered up towards the cliff. The higher he went, the more he tended to slip back as the ground beneath his feet seemed to gain a life of its own, trying to prevent him reaching his goal.

With his heart racing and chest aching as his breath whistled in and out, he at last reached a flat area just below the towering cliff – and then he saw the hole.

It was jet black, not just dark through lack of light, but a darkness which seemed almost solid. As he approached the blackness, he suddenly thought there may be something even worse than the thing which tried to follow him up the slope, waiting there. The slithery thing had now reached the flat area just behind him; he could hear it clearly. The stones rattled down the slope as it tried to reach him before he could escape.

Another few steps and he was almost touching the blackness – it seemed solid, so where could he go now?

'*Come in, you will be safe here.*' He wasn't sure if he heard it with his ears, as the voice seemed to ring in his head.

He took a step forward and reached out to the blackness. It seemed to give a little to his touch, like a huge sheet of black rubber, but then his probing fingers were pushed back.

'I can't get in!' he cried out hopelessly, as the slithering noise grew louder behind him.

'*Be willing to come in, but you must hurry.*' The voice rang in his head again. The stones behind him were rattling loudly, the creature realised its prey was about to disappear.

In desperation, Brodrick hurled himself at the blackness and it bowed inwards and then he was on the other side of it. The sound of rattling stones was no more, just an eerie silence with the occasional plop of a falling drop of water into the puddle beneath.

The walls of the tunnel seemed to give out a light of their own, faint, but enough for him to see where he was going. They were smooth, as was the floor, with the odd puddle glistening in the strange light. A few metres further in and the scene changed. The tunnel opened out with large multi-coloured stalactites hanging down from the roof and their counterpart stalagmites below.

Brodrick touched one of the stalactites as he passed it, and it rang with a faint bell like tone. Somehow he felt safe here – the air was warm and comforting as he moved forward into the ever-enlarging cavern, until there were no more walls, just a huge collection of stalactites for as far as he could see.

Brodrick stopped. Where should he go? It all looked the same, and the tunnel he had come in by was no longer visible among the forest of stalagmites.

'Come forward, you are quite safe now.' Again, that voice ringing in his head. In the distance he could see something shining brightly, the light reflecting off the circle of stalactites which surrounded it.

As he neared the brightness, he found it hard to focus his eyes. It seemed to be there, but it was so tenuous that he wasn't sure.

'Where am I?' he called out, a tinge of fear rippling through his body as he realised the alien surroundings were like nothing he had ever seen before.

'You are where many have been before and returned safely. You can return to your world should your fear be too great, but before you do, hear what I have to say.'

He stood trembling slightly as he looked at the shimmering light which seemed to pulsate in and out of existence.

'Alright, what are you, and how can you talk in my head?'

'I wish I could answer you so that you would understand, but you do not have the words or knowledge for that as of now. Perhaps you will, in time.'

'Why am I here? How did I get here?'

'You had a dream in which you reached out in a moment of stress, and I was able to contact you. I then called you here, but you did not come easily. I had to make many attempts. The reason? I wanted to communicate with you, as I have done with many others. We have much to share, if you are so willing.'

Brodrick thought for a moment; no harm had come to him so far, and he had the option of returning should he feel threatened.

'I can return home, if and when I wish?' He asked, wanting to make sure he had an escape route – although he somehow believed what the 'light' had said.

'*Yes, you can. You only have to wish it; I cannot make you stay, that would be against the principles on which I work.*'

'Alright, what do you want of me?' Somehow the fear had left him, only curiosity remained. There was a long pause before a response came.

'*As I have said, I wish to communicate with you, but not in the way you understand it. Many beings have been here, and we have exchanged our experiences and thoughts. I collect the knowledge of all beings I can contact, and in exchange I give them my knowledge and abilities. It is a mutual sharing – it benefits all concerned. Do you wish to engage in this sharing? You do not have to, but you could benefit greatly if you do, and I shall have acquired a little more of what makes sentient beings the way they are.*'

'What are these other beings you refer to? Where do they come from?' Somehow he felt he knew the answer, but he had to ask.

'*You only seem to have knowledge of your own world, but there are very many more with life on them. The universe is vast and so very varied, so vast I will never be able to reach them all in the time I have – but I must try.*'

'What do I have to do to share with you? It would take a very long time if I have to talk it all through.'

'*Just come closer and touch me – it will not hurt, you may feel an unusual sensation, but I cannot tell you what it will be. It would seem to be different for each type of being.*'

Brodrick paused for a moment; just what was he getting himself into? Would it strip him of all his memories, or were they just copied? Would he still be him after the exchange, and just what would the exchange give him? He now had more questions than ever. He waited until he felt a little calmer, and then agreed.

As he approached the 'light' it seemed to grow bigger, and then it enveloped him – totally. He reached out and touched something – it was warm and comforting in a strange way – and then he was back in his childhood. The memories raced by, all the joy and fear he had ever known, his days at school and the inevitable fights, his first real girlfriend and the pain of their parting, his work and the frustrations of not being understood, right up to the time of the dreams. There was a pause, and then a sense of things moving, odd shapes and sounds, a twisting sensation, and then it stopped.

He moved back from the 'light' a pace or two and wondered what would happen next. He felt the same, he could still remember things, but had he changed?

'Thank you for your contribution, I hope it was not too unpleasant for you. I have gained much from your memories, and I hope the enhancement will aid your survival and pleasure in life. Do you now wish to return to your home world?'

Brodrick thought for a moment – what else was there to do here? He could ask the 'light' some questions, but then doubted if he would understand the answers. Although the 'light' was able to communicate with him, it was totally alien to anything he knew about, and he was beginning to feel a bit edgy.

'If I return to my own world, can I contact you again?' He asked, hoping that he could, just in case things were not quite as he expected them to be upon returning.

'Once you leave here you cannot contact me again, but I may contact you if the need should arise. Are you willing for me to do that?'

'Yes. Alright, I'd like to go home now.'

'You will have to leave this chamber first. Just follow the light out into the open, and you will return.'

'But what about the slithery thing? It could still be out there waiting for me.' He asked, feeling real fear since meeting the 'light'.

'It will not be there; you are quite safe.' He thought he felt a slight chuckle behind the voice in his head, but thought better than to query it.

The glowing light seemed to dull just a little, and when he turned around there was a much smaller version of the 'light' just ahead of him, gently pulsing in intensity. Brodrick followed the glowing ball through the maze of stalactites and eventually came to the blackness, whereupon the ball of light just disappeared.

Taking a few quick short steps, he hurled himself at the blackness, and he was through and out onto the open plain. It was much the same, except the mist had disappeared and he could see into the far distance. On the horizon there were some dark rocky outcrops, jagged and hostile. Looking down the slope he had climbed earlier, there was nothing but gravel, small stones and the occasional lump of rock.

He stooped down and picked up a small stone, not knowing quite why, and then waited for something to happen – but it didn't – and then panic set in.

Brodrick woke up in his bed – trembling a little, and thankful the dream was over. As he rolled out of bed, he felt something hard against his thigh and looking down, saw the stone. He froze, not wanting to accept that which he knew he must. It was oval in shape, glass smooth, and seemed to be composed of countless millions of tiny specks of some multi-coloured sparkly material – quite beautiful – except it reminded him of the awful dreams, and he would rather forget that experience.

He placed the stone on the mantle above the fireplace which he had never lit, and set about making breakfast. It was the biggest fry-up he had ever made, he was ravenous - the sort of hunger he had not experienced for a very long time.

Breakfast over, the morning dragged on until it was time to go to the fast-food shop to begin the afternoon and evening shift. He didn't like it, but it was a living – of sorts. Ten o'clock came, and he gathered up his evening meal from the leftovers and set off for home.

At one point the street narrowed down and was in partial darkness, as the streetlight had failed some months ago. He didn't like this section of road, it had a nasty feel about it, and he had been mugged here twice in the past, and once got badly beaten because he had resisted.

In the middle of the narrowest part, two hooded black shapes detached themselves from darkened doorways on each side of the road and converged towards him. He felt his stomach knot up, and a surge of rage he hadn't known before.

One metre from him they suddenly stopped – no, they hadn't stopped, but had gone into slow motion, as in a dream. Brodrick quickly moved between them, turned, and placing a hand on the side of each of their heads, drove their heads together with all the force he could muster.

The sickening crackle of shattered bones echoed across the street as the two bodies slowly tumbled to the ground in a gyrating tangle of arms and legs, and lay there – still. And then he was back in real time, as the city sounds returned. There was the distant sound of a police car siren and Brodrick instinctively moved across the street to hide in a doorway – realising just what he had done. No one could blame him for defending himself, but the law being the law, it would be a messy few days as things got sorted out.

The wail of the siren drew nearer as the police car came around the corner with screeching tyres, and hit the two bodies full on. The scene seemed to freeze again, and Brodrick took advantage of this to run down the street towards his apartment.

He sat there, shaking at the enormity of what he had done. Then a feeling of relief came over him as he realised that after the car had struck the two bodies, it would be very difficult to determine just what had happened, and as far as he knew, he hadn't been seen.

Brodrick tried to fathom exactly what had happened. Was this a new ability he had been given by the 'light', and if so, what else had he acquired? It seemed that when under stress, things happened. Time, for the rest of the world, had slowed down, or had he sped up? The force he had applied to the two heads shouldn't have caused that much damage, but it had.

A stiff drink of whisky from his nearly empty bottle steadied his nerves a little while he wondered how he could check out what else he was now capable of – if anything. He wished he could return to that strange barren world just to ask a few more questions, but he knew he couldn't, so he'd just have to wait and see what happened next time he felt stressed.

It was the early hours of the morning before he could sleep; thoughts kept racing around in his head. But there were few conclusions which could be drawn from them. When he did sleep, it was deep and peaceful, and he felt refreshed and alert as the bright sunlight burst through his window next morning.

Brodrick turned on the radio and tuned in the local station for any news of interest and caught an item about two police officers, who were being investigated for careless driving. 'Poor sods,' he thought, 'it's not all their fault,' but decided not to offer any explanations, as it would leave him with questions he had no hope of answering.

He spent a good part of the morning down at the sea front sitting on one of the corporation chairs, and enjoying the cool sea breeze which drifted in. A man with a large dog walked by, and the dog stopped right in front of him and did what dogs do after a hearty meal. The man looked back but made no attempt to pick up the mess, which was against the local by-laws. The putrid smell assaulted his nostrils and a little surge of anger rippled through Brodrick. 'Irresponsible sod, clean that up,' he thought.

The man took several trance-like steps forward, stooped down, and swept the offending object up in his hand. As he straightened up, a look of startled bewilderment crossed his face. Try as he might, he couldn't shake it free, it just stuck there. Suddenly aware that Brodrick was watching him, the man turned and walked on down the sea front, still shaking his hand every now and again, and muttering incoherently to himself. The dog followed dutifully behind him, blissfully unaware that anything untoward had happened.

Brodrick sat there stunned for a moment, 'Oh God, I'm going to have to be careful what I wish for, as the old Chinese saying goes.' he thought, and then had a good laugh as he realised that justice had been done.

He frittered the rest of the morning away, being very careful not to cause any more mayhem in his vicinity, and then went in to work.

Halfway through the evening, the deep fat fryer went *woooosh*, and a pillar of flame leapt up, with coiling black clouds of smoke writhing along the ceiling. And then the scene again went into slow motion. He quickly grabbed two white coats from under the counter and threw them into the sink, and dunking them into the greasy water, wrung out most of it and draped them over the fryer. The flames went out, but the boiling oil still had plenty of heat in it, and clouds of white oil vapour continued to rise. He looked at the gas valve and it promptly shut off with a click. And then real time returned. 'How the hell did you do that?' yelled the owner, white-faced, 'you were just a blur – bloody hell, you can move fast when you want to.' Brodrick shrugged his shoulders – what could he say?

As they shut the shop down for the night, the owner thrust a bundle of notes into Brodrick's pocket, admitting he had let the insurance lapse and the quick action had saved him a fortune.

The following day, he was idly glancing through the local paper when his eyes alighted upon the horse racing pages. He had never bet on the horses because he didn't know enough about the system, but as his eyes went down the list of runners, a name attracted his attention. 'I wonder?' he thought, 'might as well give it a try.'

The horse came in at twenty to one, and he collected a nice little pile of bank notes and a scowl from the payout clerk. The next time, he placed a bet on every horse which caught his attention in each of the races. At pay out, the clerk gave him an even bigger scowl.

Brodrick had heard about an 'accumulator', where each horse's winnings is then placed on the next race, and so on, for all the races on that day. The pay out was enormous, and the manager of the betting shop asked him how he did it. 'Just good luck - and a lot of study.' Brodrick added as an afterthought.

After two more 'accumulators', the betting shop refused to take his bets. So he looked around for other betting shops. It wasn't long before these too refused him, and the betting game ground to a halt.

One evening, there was a knock on his door. Two men stood there with grim looks on their faces, one dressed in a very smart suit and the other, a Neanderthal man, dressed in clothes two sizes too small for him. Before Brodrick could ask them what they wanted, they had pushed their way into his abode and stood staring at him. 'Alright,' said the smart man, 'how do you do it?'

'How do I do what?' he replied, sensing somehow what it was all about.

'How do you get such consistent wins?' replied the smart suit. There was no way Brodrick was going to explain that.

'Well,' he answered after a long pause, 'I lay the papers down on the floor with the racing pages uppermost. I then rip some cardboard boxes up so that I can make a little wall around the papers. Next, I feed my Hamster with its favourite food, wait a few minutes and then place it in the enclosure. Whatever name the hamster craps on, I use to place a bet.'

The Neanderthal took a step forward, but smart suit steadied him with an outstretched hand. 'I can see that you need a little more time to think about this. We'll be back.' And with that the pair left.

Next day, Brodrick left his apartment and the fast-food shop, moving to a better part of town, and making sure he left no traces of where he had gone.

Although he had never been in a casino, he thought he would give it a try. Standing next to the roulette wheel, he waited until his eyes were attracted to a particular number on the board, and then placed his bet. After several consecutive wins, two 'heavies' took up position on either side of him. One more win, and he was asked in no uncertain terms to accompany them to the manager's office.

'I think you had better explain your good luck.' said the manager, 'You must be cheating, in some form or other.'

'Well, your bloody wheel's fixed,' Brodrick replied, trying to keep an even tone to voice, 'so I think that's fair.' The manager scowled at him.

'You can cash in your chips, but we don't want to see you here again. Is that understood?' Brodrick replied it was, and left.

When his bank statement came in at the end of the month, he was amazed. He had no idea how much money he had made; he was too busy making it. The only other means of increasing his share of the world's money was to invest in stocks and shares – no one could stop him from gaining wealth in that medium. As he had little knowledge of such things, he decided to study the subject, and then invest in small companies which were about to make a breakthrough in their development.

Much to his amazement, he found he could absorb and understand data at a prodigious rate, something he had never been able to do before. Was this another of his new abilities?

The investment business was a lot slower than his other enterprises in generating income, but it was steady – and worked well as long as he kept an eye on when to sell.

As his fortunes escalated even higher after a few months, Brodrick decided he would move to an even more salubrious neighbourhood, among the lesser film stars, bankers, and other moguls of industry. It was a detached dwelling in its own grounds with beautifully manicured lawns and flower beds. A man was hired to keep the grounds in good shape, and tend the swimming pool.

He felt he should now take on the attributes of one who does not have to do manual work, as it were; this included a little speech therapy, a new wardrobe, a large, new, but not flashy car, and an accountant to look after his taxes.

It wasn't long before the invitations came streaming in; most were to parties where everyone was trying to outdo the others, and he got bored with the pettiness of it.

Over time, he was able to extricate himself from the general melee that was the party scene in his neighbourhood, and collect a small group of intelligent friends with whom he could have a reasonable conversation and an enjoyable evening, and so he settled down to his new life.

A phone call from his accountant one day informed him that if he didn't 'lose' some of his money, he would find most of it going into the tax man's coffers. The suggestion was that he buy out one of the companies he had considerable shares in, as he had adequate funds to do so, and it would give the accountant a little more flexibility to manage his wealth. Brodrick agreed, and found himself the new owner of a computer software company, small but very dynamic.

A visit to the company revealed that their main source of income came from tailor-made programs for their customer's businesses, along with building computer anti-virus programs. The anti-virus part of the operation intrigued him, and he set about trying to understand the problem. As he was looking at it from a new angle it wasn't long before he came up with an idea that seemed so simple, he wondered why no one had thought of it before.

Brodrick arranged a meeting with the two top programmers and put the outlines of his idea to them. Three weeks later, the new program was in beta testing, and nothing malicious got through. A week later and the program hit the market, and the press reviews declared it a world beater. Sales went through the roof, and this in turn generated even more money – but this time it was held within the company.

Several days went by before something unpleasant happened. Brodrick had gone to bed and was in deep sleep when something woke him up. He slipped quietly from the bed, pushing the pillow into a position which made it look as if someone was still there, and took up a position just inside his walk-in wardrobe. The bedroom door opened with hardly a sound and a shadowy figure advanced towards the now empty bed. The figure raised its arm and several quiet coughs indicated that a silenced weapon had been used, the bed clothes jerking as the bullets ripped home.

Brodrick wondered what to do when time slowed down, as it did when he was threatened. Seizing his opportunity, he moved forward and delivered a rabbit punch to the assailant's neck. Slowly the figure dropped to the floor and lay there, inert, and then time returned to normal.

Brodrick put the light on and went though the man's pockets. All he could find was some loose change, a train ticket from a town some one hundred miles away and a local bus ticket. All the labels from the man's clothing had been removed – there was nothing to trace him by. 'Someone's upset,' he thought, 'and this is about as professional as it gets.' He thought there was a slight suggestion that the man had originated somewhere in Eastern Europe by his skin colour and features, but he couldn't be sure. Someone had gone to a lot of trouble to get it right, and would have succeeded if Broderick's awareness hadn't been enhanced.

As the figure hadn't moved at all, Brodrick checked for a pulse, and found none. He had unintentionally broken his assailant's neck, and now he was stuck with a dead body and a lot of explaining to do. He dragged the limp body downstairs and into the double garage where he had just installed an extra deep freezer, and unceremoniously dumped it there, to await a method of final disposal.

Returning to his bed, he tried to figure out the reason for this assault on his person; the only conclusion he could come to was that the new anti-virus program was just a little too good, and had blocked the activities of those who ran some very lucrative internet scams.

Next day he had some very sophisticated security installed – no one else would get in so easily, and if they did get into the grounds they would be recorded in glorious colour.

All was nice and quiet for a time, just the occasional visit to his new company, and a sailing yacht he had always wanted – and then one day, the company rang him up to say that they had been visited by what they thought were government officials of some kind, and would he please come down to sort it out.

Try as he might, he couldn't pin down just what department the three visitors were from – they were very evasive on that matter. What they did want, was some software which they could apply to their computer systems such that no foreign power could get in and cause mayhem. The problem seemed to be the ability of some interested parties to get past their password systems, and into the main databases.

Brodrick said that they would give it some thought, but this was not good enough for the visitors. 'You must realise that a foreign power could shut down our nuclear reactors if they can get into the systems which control them, and then we would have a cyber war which could wreck the whole planet's economy.' Brodrick thought for a moment, 'Do you mean that you already have the power to retaliate if this should happen?' The three men looked at one another, and then the senior one spoke.

'Well, yes.' came the reply, with some hesitation.

Brodrick was pensive for a while as he mulled over the implications of such a piece of software.

'Just supposing that it could be done, we would have to make it available to any nation in the world – it wouldn't be ethical to do otherwise.'

'But then we couldn't....' the senior one broke off, as he realised what he was about to say. 'There is one other problem,' he added quickly, 'the internet can be jammed if enough bogus requests are sent out, and that would leave us powerless to do anything about it.'

'You are asking an awful lot,' Brodrick replied, 'and we can't guarantee we can deliver on any of it, but we will try.'

The three men arose from their seats with grim looks on their collective faces. Someone, somewhere in a government department was very worried, and Brodrick began to wonder just what he had got himself into. It looked as if his nice, peaceful world was about to be shaken up – again.

That night, Brodrick got to thinking about the problem; at first it seemed impossible, but in his estimation if a problem existed, then it should contain the elements of its own solution. It was long past midnight before he had outlined the basic system on which the software would be built, and decided to turn in for the night, or what was left of it.

He slept well for a while, and then the dream began. He was among several others who looked human, but only just, but they seemed quite pleasant as he explained his problem. They looked puzzled at first, and began talking among themselves, although he couldn't understand a word of it. One of the strange figures nodded at the others, turned to Brodrick and smiled – at least, that was what he thought it was.

A short black stick appeared in the man's hand, and he turned to a white wall and began writing in unrecognisable symbols. Brodrick couldn't make any sense of them, but he did notice the relationship between them. And then the dream faded.

When he awoke, he grabbed a piece of paper and wrote down as many of the strange symbols as he could remember, and the order in which they had been written. He gazed at his handiwork for a while in frustration, and then remembered that the relationship between the symbols was the important part of the whole thing.

With a hurried breakfast over and steaming mug of coffee at the ready, Brodrick set about laying out the fundamentals of the new 'blocked access program.' As he went through it, he realised that without the 'dream', he would never have had the concept contained in the relationship of the symbols to each other, and wondered if the system would work on this planet, for the data he had gained certainly didn't come from here.

Two long days later and Brodrick had finished the project, now it just needed fleshing out by the company's top programmers – and testing. The other problem he had been advised of was the slowing down of the internet by mass requests to many sites, the sites crashing in the process. This was a little more difficult, as it meant getting the cooperation of all of the internet providers, and he doubted if some countries would go along with that.

A few nights later, the alarm system announced that someone or something had breached his security setup. He went to the window, overlooking the grounds and hit the floodlight switch, just in time to see two shadowy figures high-tailing it over the wall, followed by the roar of a fast receding car. He began to think he would have been better off staying at the fast-food shop – but then recalled the affluent comfort he now enjoyed, gave a sigh, and went back to bed.

The new program was now complete, and ready for its beta testing. Two major corporations were selected for the offer of something seemingly impossible, and jumped at the chance as it was free. Once installed on their systems, Brodrick asked his I.T. team to try and break into the two corporation's computer systems, as they had built it in the first place – and they were unable to.

The next step was a bit tricky – Brodrick wanted to invite anyone on the 'Net' to have a go at breaking into the two corporations. But they would not agree; he would have to wait for word of mouth to spread the good news, as most people were still sceptical that his system was foolproof.

The body in the garage came to mind occasionally, and he decided he had better do something about it – just in case it was accidentally discovered.

Disposal at sea seemed the best option, and he then remembered a headland he had once visited where the sheer cliffs dropped straight down to the ocean. If he launched the body at high tide, it should be washed out to sea before it was discovered - if at all.

His car, a large hatchback, was ideally suited for the job – he could load it while in the garage, well away from prying eyes, and it would just be a matter of waiting until he was the only one left at the cliff top before the launch.

Getting the body out of the freezer and into a plastic bag was a little more difficult than he had thought, as it was somewhat bent and rock hard. He wished he had thought about it before he had consigned his assailant to the freeze up. Eventually it was done, and Brodrick thought a little birdwatching would be a good excuse to be at the cliffs for a longish period of time – there was no telling how long others would wish to admire the stunning view.

Arriving at the cliffs in the late afternoon and armed with a flask of coffee and some sandwiches, Brodrick set about a session of birdwatching. He was surprised how interesting it was, and as dusk fell and other people drifted away, he was soon almost alone. One car remained, with the windows well and truly steamed up – faint giggles and squeals drifted across the cliff top, leaving little to his imagination.

Eventually nature was satisfied, and the lone car drove off into the darkness. He waited until he was quite sure he was the only one left, and then opened the rear hatch and dragged the now thawing body out and up to the cliff edge. Opening one end of the bag he swung it around so that it hung just over the cliff. He had carefully checked the tide times, and if he had got it right, the full tide should now be turning and would carry the body out to sea.

As the corpse was now well on its way to a full thaw, it slipped out of the bag and over the edge like so much toothpaste coming out of a tube. Brodrick listened for the splash, but it was too far down for the sound to reach him. Carefully folding the open edge of the bag back so that no tell-tail drips of the thaw could be detected on the grass, he then rolled the bag up, got into the car and drove off. He didn't like what he had done, but there was little else he could do.

That night Brodrick had some strange dreams – little of which made any sense in the morning. A hearty breakfast soon restored things back to as near normality as they were likely to get, bearing in mind what he had been through.

Two weeks later and another large corporation asked for details of the new security program – it was quickly installed, and then the rush began, as others didn't want to be left behind and open to hacking. The money flowed in.

Brodrick kept getting the idea that he should set about catching any intruders, instead of just scaring them off – as he felt sure that he hadn't seen the last of them.

The first idea was to electrify the top of the security walls such that once a 'visitor' got in, they couldn't get out again. This appealed to him, as finding the source of the problem was the only way of curing it. An electrician was hired and given explicit instructions about the system Brodrick wanted, such that entry could be achieved, and this would then power up the electrified wall top. He would have to wait a few weeks before anyone tried to invade his property, but they did, eventually.

In the early hours of the morning, the soft ding-ding of the intruder alert sounded, and leaping out of bed he went over to the security viewing screens. Sure enough, a dark figure was skulking from bush to bush, doing its best not to be seen. When Brodrick was satisfied there was only one, he hit the floodlight switch and the whole garden was bathed in harsh white light. The figure froze between bushes.

Picking up the microphone, Brodrick politely asked what the intruder wanted. It was too much, the dark figure made a beeline for the nearest section of wall and leapt up. As his hand grabbed the top of the wall, he let out a screech and fell to the ground, writing about in agony.

Brodrick flicked a switch, increasing the current in the wires, picked up a handgun and went outside to confront his intruder. Seeing him coming, the shrouded figure staggered to its feet and tried once more to surmount the wall. This time there was a faint crackle and a blue flash as the figure tumbled to the ground and lay quite still.

Brodrick gave the figure a good poke with his foot, but got no response, so assumed it was unconscious. Tucking the gun into the top of his sleeping shorts, he dragged the man by the feet towards the garage, where he had already prepared a suitable holding box for just this sort of occasion, and pushed the supine figure inside, closing the lid – and then went back to bed.

Next morning after a quick breakfast, Brodrick went to the garage to see how his captive was fairing. Opening a small door in the front of the box, he peered in. Two cold grey bloodshot eyes stared back, followed by a grunt as the man tried to clear his dry throat. Brodrick passed a plastic beaker of water laced with di-sodium thiopental into the unsuspecting man, and watched him gulp it greedily down. A few moments later, the man slowly slumped down to the bottom of the box, with only the top of his head showing.

Brodrick dragged the sleeping figure out and strapped him securely into a heavy chair. It would be some time before he reached a state of semi-consciousness, and that was the state he needed him in for interrogation.

The drug, basically a barbiturate, has the effect of decreasing the higher cortical brain function, making it easier to overcome any desire to withhold information, but it also depended on the skill of the interrogator to a large degree for its effectiveness.

Brodrick thought he had perhaps given the man an overdose, but by midday he was showing signs of a dreamy awareness, so now he could begin.

Before long, Brodrick had the man's name, and the name and address of the person who had hired him, but not the reason for the break-in. Try as he might, he drew a blank at every question and concluded that the man had been sent just to try out the degree of security Brodrick had installed.

This worried Brodrick, as it implied that another break-in was planned – possibly with more sinister intentions. He could either increase his security, leave the scene, or go on the attack. He chose attack. The man was bundled into the holding box with enough water for a few days, as he didn't know how long he would be, and the door firmly shut and locked.

Brodrick had the idea that he should take an assortment of items with him, but what? And then a list of unrelated things came to mind. These were collected up and placed in an engineer's toolbox.

Not wishing to risk his shiny new car to the possible vandalism his old home area might inflict upon it, he hired a taxi to take him to the less savoury part of town. After several discreet enquiries he managed to hire the services of two of the meanest looking heavy weights in the area; after dressing them up in smart suits, they could be mistaken for twins, with their shaven heads and bulging muscles.

One of the heavies offered the use of his Hummer, a vehicle to inspire fear or wonderment, depending upon who you were. After a briefing with strict instructions about what to do and what not to do, the trio set off in the vehicle, arriving at their destination in the early afternoon.

It was a seedy area, to say the least, and for a moment Brodrick felt a little twinge of discomfort, until he remembered his new abilities. The address took some finding as it was a shared building, but they located the correct door after a while.

There was no bell push, so a couple of hefty thumps on the door brought about the desired effect. A sour faced man in a crumpled t-shirt opened the door, and was promptly grabbed by the shoulders by one of the heavies, who lifted him up to crack his head on the ceiling of the passageway, leaving a neat dent in the plasterboard.

The man slumped down with a groan and lay still in an untidy heap. The three men raced up the stairs and burst into a dingy room containing a couple of chairs, an old desk, and a man with a look of shock on his face. As the man reached under his desk, time slowed down, and Brodrick walked up to him in time to wrest the automatic from his hand before he could level it at his visitors, then returned to where he had been standing.

The look of surprise on the face of the man behind the desk said it all, as Brodrick levelled the automatic at him.

'We need some information from you, and we aren't fussy how we obtain it.' Were Brodrick's opening words. By now, the two heavies had taken up station on each side of the seated man, looking as mean as they could. The man said nothing.

'You sent someone to check out the property of a client of ours, and he didn't like it. Oh, and your man won't be coming back. So what's this all about?'

'I don't know what you're talking about.' Came the reply, whereupon one of the heavies thrust two fingers up the man's nose and twisted them around. If the other heavy hadn't clamped the man's mouth shut, the scream would have been heard for miles. The heavy removed his fingers, wiping the blood off on the man's shirt front and giving him a smart cuff behind the head for good measure.

A little more gentle persuasion, and they got the information they wanted. The man had been hired by a company a short distance away, but had not been given the reason for the job. Brodrick took a small box from his pocket, extracted a loaded hypodermic and injected the contents into the man's arm before he knew what was happening. The man slumped to the floor behind the desk. To all intents and purposes, anyone standing at the doorway would think the room was empty.

'Cor, you don't muck about, Boss.' One of the heavies exclaimed, suitably impressed.

'Can't afford to in this game.' Brodrick replied, closing the door behind them.

They drove to the address given and found the building. It was set apart from the other rundown dwellings and was surrounded by a high chain link fence, with copious amounts of razor wire to garnish the top.

'OK,' said Brodrick, 'lets go get some food, this might take a little longer than I thought.' And with that, they left the area for some bright lights and a little sustenance. Over the meal, one of the heavies asked Brodrick what he had in mind for the fortified building. Brodrick replied that someone was giving him a very hard time and would like to see him dead, and that being the case, he thought it only right that he took the initiative.

'You gonna torch it, Boss?' one of them asked, a touch of anticipation in his voice.

'Something like that.' He replied, with a grin.

The meal finished and a round of drinks consumed, the trio set off in the Hummer for the evening's action. It was quite dark when they arrived, and there were no lights showing in the building.

'Wonder if they got a caretaker?' One of the heavies offered.

'Doubt that, what with all that high fencing and the razor wire, no one's going to fool with that.' Replied Brodrick, hopefully.

They parked in the shadow of a derelict shambles which had once been a shop, and made their way on foot to a part of the fencing which was in darkness.

Brodrick withdrew a neon lamp with two wires attached from his pocket and, holding one wire to the ground with his foot, touched the bare end of the other to the fence. The lamp flashed brightly, and they then knew the fence was electrified.

'This bunch aren't taking any chances – they must have something in there they don't want anyone else to know about.' he muttered. The heavies nodded sagely.

They went back to the wagon and Brodrick withdrew the box they had brought along. Putting a candle and a lighter in his pocket along with some lock picking tools and a small torch, he handed another torch to one of his helpers.

'One of you stay by the Hummer, the other by the fence. If you see anyone nosing about, flash the light, the other start up the Hummer – I'll hear that and exit.'

In the darkness, Brodrick lent against the Hummer and tried to think of the fence and building as being a terrible threat to him. Everything stood still, all sound stopped, and the two heavies stood motionless at the other end of the vehicle.

Brodrick hurried along the fence until he came to the gateway. This seemed to be padlocked, but to one side was a post-delivery box which drew his attention. It looked like a normal post box, and not quite knowing why, he ran his fingers around the back and found a knob. Pressing it, a flap opened up to reveal a switch. He flicked the switch up, took out the neon tester and found the fence was still live, but the gate was safe.

Using the lock picks, the gate was opened, and he headed towards the main door of the building. Again, the lock picks did their job, and he was inside. The building was on two floors, and he began to explore it. Some doors were locked, but he easily kicked them in. In one room stood four massive servers, several desks with computers on them and a lot of other equipment he didn't understand. A couple of filing cabinets revealed what he thought might be bank security codes, along with passwords of countless numbers of their customers, while another cabinet contained hundreds of credit cards, no doubt cloned. To Brodrick's mind, this was a well organised criminal setup, designed to make millions, if it ever went into full operation.

At one end of the building was a canteen, complete with a gas cooker and several small ovens. His attention was drawn to the main gas inlet pipe, which seemed much bigger than the equipment in the canteen called for. And then he knew what he had to do. Going to the other end of the building, he set the candle up in a corner and lit it. Returning to the canteen, he smashed the coupling off the main gas inlet pipe and hurried out to the main door, locking it behind him.

The door in the fence was also locked and he returned to his position by the Hummer. Suddenly, the night sounds returned.

'Hi Boss, we wondered where you'd gone, couldn't find you for a couple of minutes.'

'Just gone for a pee, I think it's time we left here.' Brodrick replied.

'But you ain't done nothing.' One of the heavies said. Brodrick remained silent.

The Hummer quietly drove off, and when they reached the top of a nearby hill, Brodrick asked them to stop.

'I can just make out the area we were in. Let's watch and see what happens.' They all stared out into the darkness, in the general direction of the mystery building.

The gas continued to gush forth from the severed coupling, drifting up into all the rooms, and then along the ground floor, towards the other end of the block.

The candle flickered once and then was no more in the ensuing blast.

From their vantage point on the hill the trio saw the vivid flash followed by a deep '*woooomph*' as the building tore itself apart. A vast column of fire writhed skyward, lighting up the neighbourhood and then settled down to consume the rest of the building and its contents.

'Gawd Boss, how did you do that?' one of the heavies asked, awestruck as the conflagration continued. Brodrick just grunted. No way was he going to explain what had happened.

The heavies returned to their home base, more than impressed, and Brodrick handed each a good wodge of notes as a bonus with the instruction that not one word of the escapade was to be mentioned to anyone, under any circumstances. They readily agreed.

Taking a taxi home, Brodrick thought that the evening's work might well put anyone else off trying to remove him, but not being certain of that, he resolved to refortify his establishment, but discreetly.

He slept well that night, and in the morning went to see the man in the box, who by now had recovered somewhat and was complaining bitterly.

'If I ever see you or any of your mates around here again, you'll end up in the concrete of that new flyover they are constructing – got it?' The man said he understood, and white faced and shaking, was escorted off the premises.

It was while Brodrick was pondering on what other hidden talents he may have acquired, that he realised that he didn't have to be actually threatened to trigger the time slip phenomenon. Now, it was just the thought of threat which seemed to work.

He decided he would get himself a new watch, and set off down town to a jeweller's shop he had seen. Approaching the shop, he heard a gun shot, and then three masked men rushed out to a waiting car, piled in, and the car roared off down the road. He looked at the car, feeling anger, and the car's engine spluttered twice, and died. The three men got out, and Brodrick didn't like the idea of their getting away, so he looked at them – and then all three seemed as if they were drunk, staggering about and totally disorientated.

Someone in the shop must have pressed an alarm, for seconds later a police car screeched to a halt, and the three robbers were taken into custody.

It was later, on the evening news that he heard someone in the shop had been fatally shot – but the police couldn't find which one had pulled the trigger, as no one was saying anything. He knew he was taking a chance, but the idea that the gunman might get away with it rankled him. Brodrick drove down to the police station and offered his services to identify the guilty man. At first they declined, but after a while, as they were getting nowhere with their interrogations, he was called in to explain how he could help.

'I'm not going to tell you how I can do this, but if you let me see the men, I'll tell you which one fired the gun.' The police were not impressed.

'We always get some bloody crank turning up on occasions like this.' One of them muttered, but the senior Officer was grasping at straws.

'Ok, let him try, we have nothing to lose.' he said, and Brodrick was led away to a room with a two-way mirror set in the wall.

'Just bring all three in, that's all I need,' Brodrick said.

Three somewhat dishevelled young men shuffled into the room, propelled by four burly policemen, and were reluctantly made to line up against the opposite wall.

'That's your man,' Brodrick announced with confidence, 'the one with the ginger hair.'

'How could you possibly know that? They were all wearing full head coverings when we caught them, there was no sign of any hair.'

'Ok, have it your own way, but that's all you've got. Split 'em up, and let ginger think the others have talked, that should do it.' Brodrick was fast losing patience with the police, although he could see it from their point of view.

The senior Officer thanked him for his contribution, and ushered Brodrick out of the station, half-heartedly offering a police car home. Brodrick politely declined, saying 'Give it a go.' He smiled and walked off to his car.

Two days later, the main gate bell rang. Brodrick, checked the viewing screen to see who it might be, was surprised to see a police car patiently waiting there.

'Come in,' he said into the microphone, and released the gate lock. The car drew up outside his front door, and a very senior policeman got out, straightened his jacket and rang the doorbell.

'How can I help you?' was Brodrick's opening gambit, knowing full well why the man was here.

'If I may, I would like to talk to you about the gunman case we had a couple of days ago. You were quite right. In the end my officers did what you suggested, and the case was resolved.'

Brodrick ushered the man in and asked him to be seated. He would have to think on his feet if he wasn't going to get himself involved in something he didn't dare explain, not that anyone would believe it anyway.

'I know you said you would not explain how you knew the guilty man, which leads me to think you must have known or seen him before, which could be looked upon as you being an accessory after the fact, so to speak.'

'I have never seen any of these men before,' replied Brodrick, his hackles rising, 'and further more, I think it's a bloody cheek of you to suggest it, after what I did for your lot. It's just a skill I have, and there's no way I can explain it to you even if I wanted to – which I don't.'

'Ok, ok, let's get down to what I'm really here for. It was the certainty with which you said what you did, that got my attention. Most of my men think it was a stroke of luck, but I'm not so sure. I think you do have a skill, and it is a skill we could use when we can't solve a case. Would you be willing, in extreme and important cases, to help us out? I don't mean the everyday stuff where we have to do a lot of groundwork to complete, just the really bad and important ones where we have next to nothing to go on. Of course, it would have to be unofficial – if this got out there would be hell to pay, and the police force would be discredited somewhat.' Brodrick could see no easy way out, put like this.

'Alright, I'll give it a go, but only when you're really stuck.' With that, the meeting broke up, and Brodrick wondered just what he had got himself into.

The sales of their new security program took off well which shocked Brodrick – the money poured in, and he wondered if that in itself would cause problems – few people like success to that degree.

During the next three months, Brodrick was picked up in an unmarked car a couple of times, whisked into the rear entrance of the police station, did his thing, and whisked out again. Several days later, he would get a phone call from the police chief, thanking him for his work.

His software company grew as it received many requests for specialised programs, most of which were passed to Brodrick for the basic layout, the software engineers then filling in the details. His fear of being attacked faded as the new security program was taken up by just about anyone dealing with money, there just wasn't any point in disposing of him now – the system just blocked the fraudsters in their tracks. Something which was not advertised was a new addition to the program – a tracking system which was undetectable by the perpetrators of fraud, but which identified them and their bases.

He had heard that a team of investigators and prosecutors had been assembled and were doing a grand job of removing those who sought to make a living by defrauding others. If this spread internationally, and someone said they thought it was catching on in other countries, the internet would be a far better place to do business.

It was while on one of his boating trips with a couple of his newfound friends that Brodrick found another benefit from his visit to the 'light', so long ago.

The weather had turned nasty with a storm brewing up, when the boom swung across too quickly for him to dodge, and he was swept overboard, sustaining a deep gash on his forearm. As he sank under the water, his heart rate dropped so low that he thought it had stopped altogether. The expected impulse to breathe in was absent, and he felt quite at peace as he drifted down in the cold blue green waters.

Looking up, he noticed a pink staining in the water above him and realised he was losing blood at a prodigious rate. There was no panic, just a calm 'better sort this out' thought, as his body turned and began the drift upwards.

Breaking surface, eager hands reached down and grabbed his limp body, hauling it onboard.

'God, I thought you were a goner there,' one of his friends said, 'you were under for ages, how the hell can you hold your breath so long?'

'Didn't seem long to me,' Brodrick replied, 'mind you, I did get a whack with the boom, suppose it must have knocked me out a little.'

'It was several minutes,' his other companion added, 'and the boat must have gone on many metres before we could drop the mainsail and bring her around. How come you just popped up alongside?'

'Must have seen the shadow underwater, and swum for it,' Brodrick replied, knowing it sounded improbable. Somehow, he knew, but didn't dare try to explain it.

The gash on his arm had closed within minutes, with only a faint line to show where it had been when he washed the blood off, and although his friends made no comment, it didn't go unnoticed. It was some time before conversation returned to near normal as they battled their way back to the mooring pontoons and retired into the club house for a hot drink. The incident was never mentioned again, and this left Brodrick feeling a bit awkward, as he noticed a slight withdrawal from his sailing friends.

All went smoothly for a few days, and then the police car turned up again, but not the usual one with all the bells and whistles, this was an old and slightly battered saloon. Brodrick felt a sense of dread – the chief usually phoned his thanks in, so this was something different.

'Thought I'd better come in person, this is likely to be a little tricky,' was the chiefs opening remark. Brodrick's heart sank.

'Ok, what's the problem?' He asked as he pointed to an armchair. They both sat down, neither looking the other in the eye.

'As you know, we have solved some really difficult cases with your help, and now some awkward questions are being asked from the prosecution service, as our success rate is so much higher than other stations. I've fobbed them off so far, but I can't satisfy their curiosity any longer; they're really piling the pressure on now. If I tell them about you that'll be the end of our little operation and the crime rate will go up again – you know what a 'by the book' lot they are.' The chief looked dejected, letting out a deep sigh.

'I could just tell them I have an unusual skill, which even I can't explain,' Brodrick suggested, hopefully. 'I could say it's just knowingness or awareness taken to a higher level than most normal people have. I could even give them a little demonstration which will rattle their heads.'

'I'm sure you could, but that's not the point – it's not acceptable police procedure, and that's what they go by. I wish they'd keep their bloody noses out of it,' said the chief, getting angry as he saw his conviction rate dropping back to normal.

'All I can do is give it some thought; in the meantime, stall 'em a bit longer, and I'll try and come up with something so that you can keep your conviction rate up.' He didn't know what he would do, but something was wriggling about in the back of Brodrick's mind – and that usually meant something would turn up.

That night he had another of his strange dreams, mainly composed of odd observations he had made over the years and bits and pieces of electrical equipment, the purpose of which didn't make much sense, but he felt it all belonged together somehow.

By dawn's early light, Brodrick was busily scribbling away on his drawing pad, trying to remember as much of his dream as possible. His main aim was to come up with some means of bypassing any lies a suspect might offer in his defence – and still remain legal.

That afternoon he made his first breakthrough. Recalling a conversation he'd had with a friend sometime ago, he noticed that when remembering events from the man's early years, he seemed to look at different areas around him, almost as if memories of similar incidents belonged to specific locations in space.

He recalled that some people could see an 'aura' around others and from this, they could reveal information about them – or so they claimed. Could these two things be related? He broke off for some tea, and while he waited for the kettle to boil, the next piece of the jigsaw fell into place.

Memories were in fact 'pictures' of things which had happened to a person, and would contain emotions, hurt and many other senses. He tried it on himself, recalling the dream when he seemed to be on that strange world of sand and gravel. For a brief moment he felt the fear again, and the cold, crunchy ground beneath his feet. He gave an involuntary shudder as the picture faded and he was back in present time.

If a 'picture' could affect him, then it must somehow impinge on his body, and therefore maybe alter his body's electrical resistance. A trip to his nearest electrical shop next day provided a sensitive test meter, and a booklet explaining how it was to be used. Brodrick attached the two-meter leads onto a couple of empty food cans and, setting the meter to its most sensitive setting, grasped a can in each hand. The metre needle registered his body's resistance, just about halfway across the scale. When he recalled the 'dream', the needle gave a very tiny kick – and he then knew he was on the right track. The signal would have to be amplified quite a bit to be effective, but he felt sure someone in his software company could find some way of doing that. That night, he rang the police chief to say he was making good progress, and in a few days should have something to show him.

The technicians at his company came up trumps, producing a box with a large meter and several controls to alter the sensitivity and swing of the needle if needed.

This time he obtained a clear indication when he recalled his dream, along with several other incidents of like nature. A quick phone call, and the police chief was at his door.

'Ok, you hold the tins, and I'll ask you some questions. I want you to lie on one question and I'll see if I can find out which one it is.' The chief looked sceptical, but did as he was asked.

'Have you ever kicked a dog?' - 'No.' The needle just slowly moved across the dial.

'Have you ever hit someone else's child?' - No.' The needle gave a little kick.

'Have you ever cheated at cards?' No.' - The needle just drifted about.

'Ok, you lied about hitting someone else's child.'

'I am surprised,' said the chief, 'yes I did. Caught my neighbour's kid pinching my strawberries, so I gave him a cuff around the head, and his father gave him another one when he heard about it.'

'Looks as if we have a lie detector then,' said Brodrick, 'but we'll have to improve it a little to make the indications a bit clearer. It seems to work on the principle that when a recalled picture of an event is 'called', the energy mass of the picture moves into the body – if you lie about it, it seems to generate a change of body resistance, and that's what I pick up.'

Brodrick produced another list of questions which he went through, easily picking out the lies with a satisfied smile on his face.

'I can see one problem though,' said the chief, 'very few criminals are going to hold these tins still – if at all. It probably infringes their rights in some way or other.'

'How about we build the sensors into an ordinary chair, the sort you'd find in any interview office? Brodrick said, sensing his dream of a usable lie detector fading.

'Yes, that sounds a good idea – the interviewee wouldn't know what's going on then,' replied the chief, 'I can just see their faces after saying 'no comment' and then being confronted with the facts – yes, I like that. How long do you think it would take?'

'Give me a few days, and I'll give you a ring.' Brodrick broke out the beer, and they spent the rest of the evening discussing the vagaries of the judicial system and how they would modify it.

A chair was shipped in from the local police station, the sensor added, and Brodrick's handyman was given the dubious honour of the first trial run, without being told the purpose of the exercise. He was amazed that his lies could be picked up so easily, and left with a worried look on his face.

For the first run of the machine in the police station, it was decided that the actual indicator would be set up behind a one way glass mirror, and the observer equipped with a microphone, so he could guide the interrogator with the right questions based on the previous answer, through a small ear piece.

The first person to be interrogated was a car thief. At first, he claimed innocence, that he was somewhere else at the time. A few quick-fire questions and he visibly crumbled under the onslaught, with a look of astonishment on his face as the details of his crime came to light. The next two were house breakers, and they too finally admitted their crimes as the evidence stacked up against them.

The police chief was delighted, and said so. What the prosecution service would say was another matter. The new system was bound to cut across someone's rights, somehow.

With the money still rolling in and his accountant working overtime trying to keep it out of the clutches of the taxman, Brodrick wondered about moving again. But why? His home was all he had ever wanted and was as secure as any place was likely to be. No, he'd stay, and perhaps plant a few more shrubs or enlarge the swimming pool.

The police chief was right, the prosecution service didn't like the clandestine nature of the lie detector, and said so in no uncertain terms. But successful prosecutions were on the up, and other stations had got wind of the setup and wanted the same. The success of the system finally got noticed by those in high places, laws were subtly changed, and Brodrick's company had to open up a new unit to manufacture the ever-increasing orders.

It was when a few corrupt police officers were caught out that trouble really began. The unions kicked up a hell of a stink, but the 'powers that be' took a firm hand in the matter and after a lot of shouting and stick waving, order and common sense was restored.

Soon the system, with a few modifications, was in use in high places, and this produced a small trickle of officials suddenly leaving their posts for the most unbelievable of reasons.

With most of the world's computer systems safe from rogue attack, and a general cleanup of those holding power in industry, the world was beginning to settle down to some serious trading and progress. There was still an imbalance between the richer and poorer nations, but Brodrick hoped in time that too would be handled.

Life was easy for Brodrick, he had all the money he wanted, a nice home, but many people seemed to shy away from him after a while. His two friends he used to sail with politely declined any invitation to his boat – they were pleasant enough, but the 'falling in the water' incident had done something, and they were never quite the same again. His software company thought he was fantastic, but they only saw him as a genius programmer – there was almost no social contact.

Brodrick began to feel lonely, not that there were no people to meet, there were – but he didn't feel as if he belonged to the average person anymore. He was different, and he knew it.

And then he had a brilliant idea. Maybe someone else had been contacted by that strange light. He built a website, plain and simple, asking one question – 'Has anyone had a dream where they are on a strange cold grey world of gravel, stone and mist, and being pursued by some slithery thing? If so, please e-mail me at…' And he gave an e-mail address beginning 'Dreamer@…..'

Next day, he had a flood of e-mail replies. Eighteen asked him what he was smoking, three of which asked him to send them a sample. Seven were just plain abusive, and three 'break away' churches which he had never heard of offered to save his 'damned soul' – at a price. One came from the very police department he had helped, warning him of the consequences of imbibing illegal substances – he hoped there was no way they could trace the web posting back to him. One lady from Moldova also had strange dreams, and offered to share them with him, along with his bed.

Several days of weird emails followed, some of which were amusing, but most were from cranks of one kind or another. And then he got the one he had hoped for.

'Hello Dreamer. I have had the dream you mentioned. I'm on that gravel plain with a slope in front of me. I go up the slope to a hole in the cliff and enter a tunnel. Inside there is a bright light which talks to me, and I too now have some strange abilities – most of which aid my survival, but some are a bit frightening. I would like to meet you – we have, I think, a lot more in common than we realise. Signed, Dreamer Two.'

Brodrick wrote back, asking where they should meet, and when. The surprise was that Dreamer Two was in Australia, and offered to come to him. After several more emails, a date and time was arranged that Dreamer Two would arrive at Brodrick's nearest airport, and would be waiting at the bureau de change, dressed in a grey suit.

On the appointed day Brodrick parked his car at the airport car park, raised his eyebrows at the parking fee, and felt sorry for those who could ill afford the exorbitant cost.

Making his way through the seething throng of overheated humanity, he wondered if soap had also become a luxury. There was one lone figure at the bureau de change, dressed in a smart grey suit with dark blond hair – and it was a female.

Brodrick's heart skipped a beat – his luck was really in; he hadn't given much thought as to the sex of the other dreamer, assuming it must be a man for no particular reason. She was not exactly pretty, but attractive, he thought. And then clamped down on 'thinking', just in case she could pick up his thoughts.

As he strode towards her, she smiled – and that was when his heart went into meltdown. Her whole face beamed with pleasure as she extended a welcoming hand to the fast-approaching Brodrick. Their hands touched, and to him, it seemed as if an electric charge had passed between them.

'Hello, my name is Sally.' She said. To Brodrick it sounded like the soft rustle of silk – and he just stood there with his mouth open.

'Sorry,' he said, 'I was a bit surprised – thought it would have been a man – don't know why. Anyway, my name's Brodrick, or Brod for short, and I'm delighted to meet you.' Somehow, he didn't want to let her hand go – in case the dream faded.

'You must be tired after your journey, I've booked two rooms in a nice hotel nearby; so shall we go there, and you can freshen up, and then we can think about some tea.'

'Sounds good to me.' She replied, still smiling. Brodrick took hold of the wheeled travel case and they headed for the car park.

The hotel was old but opulent, and in prime condition, something from an age long gone. Although Brodrick was quite happy with the modern world, he did appreciate the quality and attention to detail that still existed in such places.

Reception was polite and dignified as the pair signed in and accepted their keys. Two bell boys appeared out of nowhere and whisked their cases away, while a liveried man of senior years courteously ushered them towards the lift.

Brodrick sat on the edge of his bed, still trying to come to terms with what had happened. He had wanted someone of similar ilk to himself to share his life with, but this was more than he had expected. He could feel the power of his new companion, something he had never felt in anyone else, and wondered if he was a match for such a person.

A discreet tap on his door broke him out of his trance-like state, and the door opened.

'Ok if I come in?' she asked, 'we have nothing like this where I come from – more's the pity. I could get used to this. How about that tea you mentioned?' Brodrick's knees felt weak as he arose from the bed to greet her – and he didn't know why.

They went down the marble staircase with its deep mahogany handrail and into the lounge, selected a quiet corner and sat down. A waiter materialised and afternoon tea was ordered.

'We have a lot to talk about,' she began in her soft Australian accent, relaxing back in her chair, 'and I'm not quite sure where to begin. How about you tell me what new abilities you have, and how they have affected your life?'

Brodrick suddenly felt at ease – all the tension had melted away and he too relaxed. He began with the visit to the cave, and then went through all the incidents where his new skills had come into play, right up to the present day.

'Well, you've had a more exciting time than I,' Sally said when he had finished, 'my main problem has been that people seem to sense that I'm a little different, and tend to shy away. Perhaps I have been a little more cautious with my abilities than you have. I do have some different ones though. The main problem is not generating wealth – that's easy, it's finding the happiness to go with it.'

Brodrick felt sorry for her, and then realised they were both in the same situation. They talked on for hours, exchanging experiences and ideas until it was time for dinner, which was well above his expectations.

The hotel sported a small ballroom, and after letting their meal settle down, they found themselves in each other's arms in the dim light and soothing music. Brodrick had never felt so at ease with anyone, let alone a woman – and he realised just what had been missing all those years.

Close to midnight the little orchestra played the last waltz, and they found themselves entwined like a couple of young lovers.

'That was the best evening I have ever spent,' said Brodrick, as they left the ballroom 'and I wanted it to go on forever.'

'I don't see why it shouldn't,' Sally replied, with a knowing smile, 'after all, there are only two of us, as far as we know – so neither of us need fear a rival.'

They paused outside their twin rooms. Both knew what they wanted, but both hesitated just long enough for Brodrick to fill the awkward gap with 'See you in the morning Sally.'

'Can't wait.' She replied, a little wistfully.

Over breakfast next day, the gloves came off.

'Ok, let's cut the nonsense,' began Sally, in a business-like tone, 'we both know where our meeting will lead - it's inevitable, if you think about it. Whether we marry or just live together is immaterial – we are now an item, there's no getting away from it.'

'Can't say I want to get away from it,' replied Brodrick, with a grin, 'I just wish we hadn't wasted last night.'

On their way to Brodrick's house they discussed many things, among which was what their progeny would be like.

'I think there has been a genetic change – remember my arm? Human flesh just doesn't heal that fast on its own.' Brodrick stated.

'And not only that, the scars I picked up as a child have all disappeared – normally that would take plastic surgery, they were quite extensive, and my deformed foot has straightened out – can't tell it from the other one now.' Sally added.

'You mean you have two left feet now?' He retorted, with a grin.

Within days they had settled in like a couple who had been married for years; the neighbours just took it for granted that they were a couple. Not that they had any deep social connections with those on either side of them, but they did meet on the occasional local 'get together', and got on just fine.

Somewhere on another world, in a cave deep inside a cliff, a strange light did its version of a little chuckle.

'*It is such a lovely world compared to some, perhaps now they won't destroy it.*'

BLACKNESS

On Mount Palomar, the huge dome of the observatory swung around to its pre-set position, to begin the night's study of a small star cluster C771, which had been under observation for several weeks now.

Nothing too unusual about that, except when the star cluster was looked for, it wasn't there. All the other stars were, shining just as brightly as they had done the night before, but where C771 should have been, there was just blackness.

The first thing they did was to check that there was nothing mechanically wrong, and when that was proved negative, a slight feeling of panic set in.

The dome was realigned, but C771 was still missing. The image was sent out to several other screens so that others could evaluate the situation, and then someone noticed that one of the missing stars suddenly popped into view, while another star on the fringe of the cluster faded from sight.

The conclusion was that the blackness was moving. Slowly but surely, the rest of the missing cluster came into view, while other stars on the edge of the cluster were becoming obscured. And then the blackness stopped moving.

Three other observatories were contacted and asked to pass their comments. All replies were the same, 'We can see it, but don't know what it is.' An urgent message was sent to the Pentagon, and within two hours a group of high officials, plus the usual sprinkling of high-ranking military personnel, arrived at Mount Palomar.

They observed the strange phenomena, looked at each other worryingly, but said very little.

Two weeks later and the blackness was the size of the moon, obliterating the stars behind it, but still giving no clue as to what it might be. It seemed that the object was on a collision course for Earth, and no one knew what to do about it.

For once, all the major nations forgot their differences and decided to co-operate in order to handle whatever it was coming their way. Various groups started up claiming it was the coming of the Lord, while others thought it was a visit from another race, come to save Earth from its own follies. Meetings were held and huge profits were generated, as gullible people divested themselves of all their worldly goods in order to be pure and clean when the great event happened.

The stock markets went up and down as frantic traders tried to make a killing on the fluctuations, which they themselves had generated. The blackness had stopped moving and was now in orbit around the Earth, at about the same distance as the moon, and still there was no clue as to what it could be.

The space station sent a small, manned module out to investigate, but when it was fifty or so kilometres away from the menacing object it veered away, as though it had been deflected by an invisible screen. And that's when the real panic set in. They could see it, radar beams were just deflected, as were two photographic probes, and they had no idea of its density. No instruments would give a reading which made any sense. It just hung there in space, black, menacing and motionless – and no one could do a thing about it.

Another quasi-religious group set itself up, its leader claiming that the blackness had contacted him directly, and everyone must worship the blackness at precisely six o'clock each evening – those failing to do so would be consumed by fire when the blackness descended to Earth, which it was about to do any day now – of course, those attending the mass 'pray ins' had to pay a fee.

Nothing much happened for several days, except general pandemonium among the members of a quickly assembled group of individuals, representing the major nations of Earth.

And then most countries reported a number of bright lights roaming about, a few metres above the surface of the ground, dropping down every now and again, as though they were looking for something.

Attempts were made to capture the floating lights, but they always seemed to anticipate the move, and accelerated upwards, only to descend somewhere else.

Reports then came in about the holes. It would seem that the lights were taking samples of the ground, leaving neat holes where the earth had been removed – some even taking samples of an airport's concrete runway. This, when it reached the public domain, began another round of speculation as to what the blackness intended, and more panic ensued.

The military were all for sending an atomic tipped missile up to the blackness, but were dissuaded from doing so, as all attempts to approach the invader resulted in their probes being deflected, and there was no telling where the missile would go after deflection.

All was quiet for a while. The lights had disappeared after taking their samples, and the latest speculation was that the blackness was about to denude Earth of its soil.

A few days later and the first of the cylinders appeared. Arriving in groups of twenty, they skimmed along just above ground level, descending every now and again to do something, and then rose up again to descend a half metre or so further on. A quick inspection of the ground where the cylinders had landed only revealed a slight circular depression, but the ground didn't seem to have been disturbed other than that.

There were a few sightings of the rows of cylinders a few hundred metres offshore, and several over lakes, but there was no trace of what they had done. Two days later, and storm clouds gathered over the various land sites visited by the cylinders. Gentle rain began to fall for a while, and then the skies returned to their normal blue.

A close watch was kept on those sites which the cylinders had visited, and several days later a new wave of panic hit the powers that be. Small green shoots pushed up from the damp earth, but they were like no shoots Earth had ever seen before. The first reaction was to spray each patch with a defoliant, or anything else suitably noxious, but a small group within the international committee suggested restraint. 'Let's see what the shoots turn into, it may give us a clue as to the purpose of the blackness.' And so, the shoots grew on.

The first sign of danger was when a fisherman reported huge floating mats of vegetation nearly half a metre high, surrounded by dead fish. Not only that, something was crawling about on top of the mat. The fisherman was none too keen to get close enough to see exactly what it was, saying that it appeared to be about a metre long, dark green in colour and no visible sign of legs.

To compound the situation, a sighting of something similar was seen on a floating mat on a lake, only this time the creature was grey, smaller, and with two eyes on stalks. The ground-based plants were growing at a prodigious rate, but they were no longer green. Each row was different, some had spikes in place of leaves, some had leaves like sword blades, but the most numerous seemed to be variations on what looked like balls of threads, all twisted and intertwined.

Groups of men in protective clothing enthusiastically sprayed them with a mixture of weed killing solutions. Some plants seemed to wither on contact with the spray, while others appeared to absorb it and visibly grow, according to one report.

Flame throwers were brought in to tackle those plants which were resistant to the sprays, and most of these burned readily, issuing forth thick black clouds of oily smoke from the plant oils they had produced.

Even some desert areas had sprouted strange plants, but most had died when the damp sand had dried out.

The general consensus of the international committee was that the blackness was trying to populate the Earth with strange plants as a food source prior to colonising the planet with God knows what – and no one was willing to speculate on that.

On one lake, they had managed to throw a hooked line out and dragged the floating mat of vegetation ashore, where upon it had withered and died. Just to make sure, when it had dried out, they set fire to it, but there was no sign of the bug-eyed creature that had been seen earlier.

What worried the committee most was what was happening in those areas far from civilisation, where the alien growths could grow unhindered. Satellite pictures showed some areas of the planet where the native vegetation had died back, and in the centre of which grew the alien plants. Where they could, aircraft were sent in with sprays and later with napalm bombs to burn off that which was left.

It was a losing battle, whatever it was which was trying to replant Earth, it was slowly winning, despite man's best efforts.

The next concern of the committee was a possible retaliation from the blackness for the decimation of those alien crops which had been found, so a close watch was kept on those areas which had been sprayed and fire-bombed. But one area had been left to mature just to see what would happen.

The middle row of a long line of plants had all sprouted tall stalks, atop of which pods were forming. A very close twenty-four hour watch was kept on them, flood lights being used during the hours of darkness, just in case they missed something important.

For three days the pods grew on, and then the top of each pod peeled back and a small beetle-like creature crawled out, spread its wings to dry them, and then flew off to visit the plants on either side of the row from which it had emerged. Soon there was a flurry of beetles, darting about looking for plants which hadn't been visited by another beetle, and after a while, those unfortunate enough not to find a virgin plant dropped to the ground and, as far as anyone could tell, died.

Several newly emerging beetles were caught in nets and transferred to jars, along with some dead ones for later study.

The plants which had received a visiting beetle responded by producing bulbous lumps on their stalks, and this was too much for the observers, who relayed the news back to the committee. The committee decided it was too risky to let things develop any further and ordered the flame throwers in.

Two days later and the lights returned, no doubt to check on the progress of the planting. Again, vain attempts were made to try and catch a light, but nobody managed to. The next day a rod-like thing appeared, as long as a row was wide, and proceeded to slowly drift along the row of blackened plant stems, the ground behind it steaming as whatever it was using turned any moisture in the soil into water vapour. At the end of the row, the rod zoomed up vertically and disappeared from sight.

All the dead stumps had disappeared, and a close inspection of the ground which the rod had travelled along had been cooked to a depth of about half a metre.

The following day the cylinders returned, did their little dance and then left. That night the clouds gathered, and it rained. Soon the shoots appeared, and the committee's general panic level went up another notch. The new batch of shoots were destroyed as soon as they had reached a few centimetres in height, and a watch set up for any signs of a return visit from the blackness's planting machines.

Using the satellite pictures, teams of nervous observers searched for the dreaded signs of alien planting, and when found, decontamination teams let rip with defoliant sprays, followed by fire.

A fishery patrol vessel reported a vast floating mass of something just a few miles off the coast, and a decontamination team was promptly dispatched to investigate.

The floating mass of vegetation was about half a kilometre long and nearly as wide, and stood about two metres above the sea level. It slowly heaved and rolled with the motion of the waves, giving the apparentness of having a life of its own. An inflatable was launched, along with a three-man crew, dressed in protective clothing and a diver to get a closer look at the underside of the alien invader.

As they approached the floating mass, the diver volunteered to see what lay beneath. He was gone so long the others began to panic, and then he surfaced, frantically swimming towards the inflatable.

Back on board, and his face mask removed, he related what he had seen.

'You don't want to go down there,' was his opening remark, 'it's frightening. There's a forest of tendrils as thick as my arm going right down to the ocean floor, where they have latched onto anything they can get hold of. Not only that, the tendrils on the leading edge of the thing are reaching out and dragging the whole mass slowly along. They must be absorbing minerals from the rocks, because behind the mass there's nothing but barren sand. Everything has been consumed, rock, stones, seaweed, coral – everything.'

Shocked looks went between the rest of the party, and it was decided to try and climb aboard the floating mass, if it didn't pose a threat to their presence.

With the inflatable safely tied to the edge of the floating island, two of the team hauled themselves up the two-metre high edge, and were in for another surprise.

A few metres in from the edge, long stalks had grown up, and on top of each stalk a two-metre wide balloon-like object bobbed about in the faint breeze. There were hundreds of them, stretching off into the far distance. The surface of the mass seemed to be composed of a tangle of thick brown strands, underneath a layer of green grass like filaments, but not like any grass they had ever seen.

One of the men approached one of the stalks and slashed it with a knife, severing the rest of the stalk and the balloon which shot up into the air at an astonishing speed, soon disappearing from sight. As the knife sliced through the stalk, they all heard a high-pitched squeal and the severed end of the stalk exuded a thin, pale brown liquid in a series of pulses.

'Don't do that again,' the other man said, 'the bloody thing might be more alive than we think.' He had been standing still while his companion had been busy with the knife, and when he tried to move, he found the green surface of the mass had crept up over his protective boots, and he had to use considerable effort to free himself.

'Keep moving,' he yelled out, 'if you stay still, you'll find yourself anchored to the surface. We'll go just a bit further in, and then we'll report back to the ship.'

A few metres on and they saw a head with two unblinking, malevolent black eyes suddenly protrude from the surface. The mouth opened to reveal a neat row of very sharp teeth and a warning hiss. Both men stopped in their tracks and froze.

'I think we'd better get off this bloody monstrosity before it decides we're edible.' And with that, the two men returned to the inflatable, which took off at high speed to report to the main ship. A quick consultation with the senior members of the team and they thought it might be worthwhile to try the defoliant, and if that worked, apply the flamethrowers.

The main ship edged closer to the floating mass, staying a few metres from the actual edge, and the pumps were started up. The first jet of defoliant hit the surface a few metres in, and the reaction took them all by surprise. The surface heaved itself up in a series of undulating waves, and after a few seconds, seemed to boil and froth as if the defoliant had been strong acid. Again, that strange high-pitched sound, almost as though the mass had cried out in agony.

The crew emptied the defoliant tanks as they slowly moved around the huge floating mass, and wondered what to do next, as the stricken surface seemed to have turned to a slimy substance, and therefore the flamethrowers would have no effect on it. The ship held position for several minutes, as the team tried to think of anything else they could do to halt the growth of the floating menace, the upshot of which was to return to base, report what they had found, and pass the problem on to higher authority.

The engines revved up, the ship gave a shudder, and the engines died to idling speed, as the propellers refused to turn.

'Hey, we're being pulled in,' someone yelled out, and they all rushed to the side of the ship, to see the gap between them and the floating mass of alien vegetation slowly diminishing. Two divers were hurriedly dispatched with long knives, to see what had happened below the ship. A tangled mass of tendrils had engulfed the propellers, with long strands reaching back to the main mass of the floating island. There was no way the divers could free the half-hidden propeller blades, so they cut the rope-like strands joining it to the island and resurfaced.

When onboard, they related what they had seen, and the engines were tried again. The propellers turned and the ship edged slowly away from the island. It was only when they were at a safe distance from the mass, that they tried repeatedly reverse and forward motion to the propellers, which gradually freed them from the entangling strands.

The committee, when they got the report from the ship and realised that only the edges of the alien mass had been treated, ordered mass production of defoliant. Huge fortunes were being amassed by the companies concerned in production, and those who had the foresight to invest in them.

Satellite mapping provided the whereabouts of all large masses of the menace on land and sea, and for once, every country concerned co-operated fully with the program of destruction.

A larger ship, equipped with more powerful pumps and a copious supply of defoliant was sent out to the partly destroyed floating alien island. When they got there, things had changed; the outer edges had turned to a gel like substance, and fish were greedily gulping it down as fast as they could. Even two whales were seen scooping up huge quantities of the gloop, as they cruised up and down the side of the floating mass.

A radio message was sent back to the committee relating what they had seen, and after much discussion, it was decided that the ship should stand by, try and catch some fish which had been feeding on the alien mass, and send them back for analysis.

Many days later, the ship was given the go-ahead to spray whatever they could reach of the remaining island, and then stand by again to see what happened. Going in bow-first, so that the propellers were furthest away from the mass, they noticed the sea was alive with fish of every kind, and all the gel like substance had been consumed.

Even more whales had joined the feeding frenzy, slowly cruising around at a distance, as if waiting for the ship to provide them with more of the same.

The pumps wound up to screaming pitch, and the defoliant jetted out over the floating mass of alien vegetation. Within seconds, the crew had their hands over their ears, as the island mass where the spray had reached writhed and fumed. Someone without permission, but who thought it would be good fun, fired a flare out over the island.

As it curved down from its long flight, it brushed against one of the balloons which promptly burst with a vivid flash, and a huge flame leapt skywards. After much thought, it was decided that the balloons contained hydrogen or some other light and flammable gas, and somehow helped the island stay afloat. This now became a new sport, until all stocks of flares had been exhausted.

Word came back a few days later that the fish sent in for analysis didn't seem to be harmed by what they had eaten, and when consumed by animals, and later humans, proved just as nutritious as normal. The committee announced that they thought that they were getting the upper hand at long last, and fish stocks would increase due to the new food supply. One small group within the committee even suggested that one island should be kept as a breeding stock, so that small portions could be cut off and new islands started to boost fish stocks – but no one could figure out a way of cutting off pieces to do this – so the idea was shelved, for the time being.

The main concern of the committee was that if the fish had ingested the gloop, would it affect them genetically, as the substance was so alien? Although the fish which had been consumed seemed to be harmless, only time would tell. A later report from the labs had checked on the fish DNA, and could find no change from normal, so it was thought that when the alien vegetation had broken down, any alien DNA had also been destroyed.

A bright young man, determined to go down in history as someone with more than one brain cell, had constructed a large steel box with an open bottom and a thick glass window in the top. This was suspended by a small crane, a couple of metres above a hole where a light had taken a sample, in the hopes that a cylinder would oblige him by trying to plant something there.

Sure enough, a few days later a line of cylinders hove into sight, lowered themselves down to just above ground level, and proceeded to do their planting dance. At the right moment, the suspended box was dropped on the unsuspecting cylinder as it touched the ground, and man had captured his first alien object.

The cylinder rattled and banged about in its confining box, and then eventually all was quiet. A quick look through the glass top revealed the cylinder lying on the ground, motionless. The box was raised a centimetre or so, and a steel plate slipped underneath it – a couple of quick welds, and the cylinder was now completely trapped.

Word must have got around about this venture, because before the bright young man could figure out just what he was going to do with his capture, a group of officials commandeered the box and its contents, and departed with hardly a thank you.

Inside an underground concrete bunker, a group of scientists and military, all dressed in protective suits (the military armed to the teeth), removed the holding welds and lifted the box up. The cylinder just lay there on the metal base plate – inert.

One brave person moved forward, and gingerly took hold of the cylinder.

'I can just hear a faint humming sound, and it is vibrating very slightly,' he said, turning it over in his hand, 'there appears to be some faint circular marks on what I think is the bottom, but apart from that it is featureless.'

The cylinder was tapped, shaken and x-rayed. A drop of strong acid didn't even mark the surface, and then someone produced a diamond tipped drill. The scream produced set everyone's teeth on edge, as the high-speed bit skidded about on the impenetrable surface, and the driller was told to desist. The cylinder remained unmarked.

When all else fails, use brute force. An oxy-acetylene welding torch was produced and fired up. The cylinder was placed on the concrete floor and the flame applied.

Nothing much happened, except that the cylinder began to glow a little, and just as they were about to give up, it burst into the brightest light they had ever seen, with soft sizzling sound. It was several minutes before anyone's eyesight could make out anything apart from the blinding whiteness, and then they saw the circular depression in the concrete floor – and that was all.

There was a lull in sightings of lights and cylinders for a time, even the rod-like 'ground cookers' failed to show up, so everyone wondered what would happen next.

Slowly but surely, the floating mats of alien vegetation were sprayed into oblivion, and the land sown patches were succumbing, as and when they were found. The main fear was that a few patches would be missed, and then propagate unseen to cause more trouble in the future.

The blackness was still in place, and the military were putting pressure on the committee to release a nuclear warhead above the alien structure, the idea being that with that amount of energy release the deflecting shield would fail, but not wanting to instigate any form of retaliation, they adamantly refused. The fact that it had a protection shield meant that sentient beings were in control, according to the military, and therefore was a threat to all mankind. The counter argument was that the shield was to protect it from meteorites and other space rubbish, which seemed the more likely, according to the committee.

The little beetle-like creatures which had been captured earlier didn't prove very helpful in finding out what was going on. Those which were alive at capture had died shortly afterwards, and dissection only showed that they were just little beetle-like things. Only one item of interest showed up, and that was a long sting-like appendage at the rear end, which the scientists concluded was to inject something into the plants – perhaps to fertilise them.

One or two disturbing reports came in about animals being abducted, and an unconfirmed story of two humans who went missing with no trace. It would seem that a large floating object appeared out of nowhere, and scooped them up, but there was no photographic evidence or reliable witnessing of the events, so it was put down to general hysteria and the desire to get some publicity.

Those lakes which had been seeded with the floating vegetation caused some worry, as all fish stocks in them had disappeared. There was no trace of fish having ever been present – no small fry or even a few fish bones. No one was sure if the alien plants or the spraying had destroyed them, so the sea areas where floating mats had been seen were checked for fish. They were thriving – huge shoals of all the popular breeds were present; according to some fisherman, more than they had ever seen before. This was put down to the gloop produced when the floating islands had been destroyed, and the fish had feasted on it. But why the shoals should be so big, was anyone's guess.

One disturbing report came in of a relatively small but popular fishing lake, which had a small rocky island in its middle, adorned with a mixed collection of trees and shrubs – or it used to have.

The floating alien mass of vegetation had somehow covered the island. Even the trees had been absorbed, so it now looked like a large green hump in the middle of the waters, and there were no fish to be found. An observation post was set up to monitor its progress and ordered to report in daily.

Little seemed to change for a while, except that the floating vegetation slowly grew to cover the entire surface of the lake, and then it stopped. A week later, and the observers noticed a tall spike of growth in the middle, where the island had been. This continued to grow, until it reached an estimated height of some thirty metres or so, and then it sprouted a large pod-like extrusion at the top. It was thought this might be a seed pod of some kind, and so its removal was ordered.

A local tourist had apparently walked, unharmed, halfway across the mass before anyone could stop him, so a couple of volunteers offered to remove the offending item, but only if they could use detonating cord, as they didn't fancy standing on the floating mass while trying to saw the column down – it was too thick and would take too long, and the mass might object.

A camera crew assembled to record the event, along with a few dignitaries and a spattering of military, and then the demolition team strode purposefully towards the column, armed with the explosive cord, detonator, primer, and a length of wire. It had been decided to fire the explosive electrically for safety's sake, as no one knew how the growth might react. The cord was wrapped around the trunk of the column, near its base, and the demolition crew returned, paying out the wire behind them, connected it up to the firing box and awaited their next instruction.

One of the military, adorned with copious amounts of gold braid, stepped forward and pushed the button. There was a bright flash, a very sharp bang, the column teetered for a moment and then came crashing down, the whole mass of floating vegetation rippling with the impact. Nothing else happened, so after a while they all left the site, except the observers, who were told to keep a sharp lookout for any changes.

Over the next few days, the surface of the mass grew darker in colour, but little else changed. And then tendrils began to sprout from the edges where it met the land, slowing creeping into the surrounding reeds and grass, which promptly died and were ingested.

The spray and flamethrower teams were called in to do their thing, burning the encroaching tendrils on the edge of the lake and then spraying the main body of the mass starting from the centre. Within a couple of days, the lake was just a huge puddle of jelly-like gloop, but as there were no fish to eat it, it remained so for several more days, and then it turned a dirty brown, and stayed that way.

Earth was to see no more of the alien planting system; the blackness had diminished in size and was last seen heading out of the solar system at an ever-increasing rate.

The conclusion of the committee was that the blackness was some sort of alien device, probably an automated machine, which went roaming around the universe looking for planets on which to plant its strange seeds - the purpose of which no one could work out, although a few bizarre ones were put forward, but which made little sense when looked at rationally.

Deep in the Amazon rain forest, a natural clearing had been visited by the planting machines. A troupe of small monkeys whose natural diet consisted mainly of berries and fruit, found the tender little shoots of the alien plants a real treat, and had set up home near the plot so they could partake of the juicy morsels each morning.

As chance would have it, they didn't crop the shoots right down to the ground, so the plants were able to produce new shoots the next day. After a few weeks, the monkeys broke off sticks from the smaller forest trees, and built a fence around the crop so that other creatures couldn't steal their new food source.

Well-fed monkeys equal happy monkeys, and happy monkeys tend to copulate rather a lot, so the troupe quickly grew in number - and not only that, the offspring seemed to be a little larger than their parents, when they matured.

Before long the monkeys had divided up into little groups, each having a specific job to do. One group tended the garden, keeping weeds down on the edge of the plot and gathering leaf mould to feed the alien plants, while another group's job was to keep the fence in good condition (and had added a small, simple gate) so that the other denizens of the forest could not steal their favourite food.

Eventually the alien plants, because they couldn't go into their seeding phase, gave up the unequal struggle, and died. The monkeys now had to resort to finding their old foods, and were none too happy about it. But by now, they were nearly two metres tall and walked on their hind legs most of the time; some, when searching the forest for food, marched in line and in step.

Their main predator, the Jaguar, was having a hard time of it trying to add them to its diet, as they usually travelled in small groups, and were armed with sharpened sticks. Often, it was the Jaguar who had to retreat from this new breed of monkeys.

Their other main adversary was the black Cayman, who would lay in wait on the riverbank to snatch any unwary passerby; but at the first sign of an open jaw, a shower of sharpened sticks would fill it's gaping mouth, and the Cayman soon learned to leave them alone.

A small group from a native tribe encountered the monkeys one day, and tried to capture one. Only one of the group survived to tell the tale, and he wasn't believed.

The monkey troupe now numbered some one hundred and fifty armed and intelligent males, and a slightly smaller number of females. Speech of a sort had developed, and they feared nothing in the rainforest.

BRIGHTLIGHT

IN THE SMALL fishing village of Culmouth, with its pretty little row of cottages nestling around the small harbour, a mother and son watched the brilliant display of the Perseids meteorites shower as they hit the Earth's atmosphere in a dazzle of sparkling lights.

'Wow, that's a big one,' said little Billy, as a pale green streak of light raced across the sky in front of them, emitting a faint sizzling sound. The meteorite continued its journey to Earth's surface, gently curving down until it struck the wooden covering of a dairy farm's waste pit. The farmer had dug a deep pit to take the waste from the farmhouse, toilet and the cowshed through some old clay pipes he had found. Quite an innovation, for those days.

There was a sharp crack as the wood splintered under the impact, and another as the white-hot missile struck the surface of the slurry and shattered. Deep inside the meteorite, and almost at the point of destruction due to re-entry heat, the spore was freed from its aeon's-long confinement.

For a short while, the spore just drifted around in the thick brown liquid, and then it sensed a small amount of nutriment. A mouse had got a little too close to the edge of the cover where there was a little gap, and had fallen in. The spore edged closer and detecting animal tissue, extended a pseudopod which gently probed around until it found a break in the skin, and then entered the mouse's body.

The tip of the pseudopod exuded an enzyme which broke down the mouse tissue, and the spore drank in the nutriment greedily. It had been a long time since it had received any nourishment. Slowly the spore grew in size, the cells duplicating and then changing until the entire mouse had been consumed; but it was still hungry.

The spore had now become a blob, an alien organism designed to survive under the most extreme circumstances, and it was very good at it. A series of cilia were extruded, enabling blob to swim around in the slurry, and after a thorough search of the pit, blob decided there was nothing else there for it to consume, and so sought a means of escape.

Ever since the pit had been first filled with waste, a small crack in one wall had leaked the brown liquid out into the surrounding ground, and this had found its way through tiny fissures in the subsoil to the nearby pond, which the farmer had constructed, stocked with trout, and then rented out to local fishermen. This had never been a problem, as on its journey to the pond all the solid matter had been filtered out, leaving nearly pure water to trickle through.

Blob found the crack, and began the transformation into a thread-like state, slipping through the crack and down the tiny channel towards the fishing pond. A few worms were encountered on the way, but they couldn't be consumed in blob's present state, and so they lived on, unaware of the fate that could have befallen them.

When the thread reached the pond, it reformed itself into the blob shape it had been in before, and resumed its hunt for nutriment. The pond held an abundance of trout, but blob couldn't catch them, they moved too fast. So, it resorted to scouring the lake bottom for anything which had died and lay there inert.

A frog, which had died of old age, and a couple of trout which a fisherman had thrown back as being too small for a meal, provided one for the blob. Even the bones were broken down and absorbed. Blob didn't waste good nutriment.

It had now grown to the size of a small trout, developing a sucker like mouth part and two driving fins, but it didn't look anything like the trout it had been feeding on.

Blob was still no match for the larger trout, but a couple of the smaller ones became too curious, and the sucker-like mouth locked on, a thin probe punctured their skin injecting the dissolving enzyme, and blob grew that little bit bigger. It then grew two more driving fins and a retractable barbed probe just above its mouth; now any small fish could be speared and consumed with ease.

Having gained bulk and strength, blob went for one of the bigger trout; having driven in the barb, retracted it, and got a grip with its mouth; but the fish proved too strong. A quick flip with its tail, and the trout was gone, minus a sizeable chunk out of its side. In time the trout would die, so this too would be added to blob's food source when it sank to the pond bottom.

The next development was a stunning poison added to the barbed probe. This would instantly paralyse any prey encountered, so once speared, escape was very unlikely.

Blob was now the top predator in the pond, and the fish stocks were being depleted at an ever-increasing rate.

One day a fox came down to drink, but before it could jump back from the sudden movement in the water, the paralysing barb had done its work, and fox was dragged down to the murky bottom. Its body swelled up as the dissolving enzyme went to work, and then deflated as the nutrient soup was ingested. All that was left were some tuffs of red brown fur and the claws, the teeth having been dissolved for the minerals they contained.

The first outward sign of trouble came from complaints made by the fishermen to the farmer; they had paid to fish for trout, but there were very few left and they wanted their money back. One fisherman said he hadn't caught a fish for several days, and when he cast his line there was never a tug on it, but when he pulled it up the bait had gone.

Shortly after the fishermen had withdrawn from the pond, three of the farmer's sheep went missing, and when he moved them to another field nearer the farm and replaced them with cows, one of them could not be accounted for at milking time.

Blob had now grown much bigger and stronger, and soon there was no life left in the pond apart from an amorphous ghostly shape which skulked along the bottom of the lifeless waters, wondering where the next meal was coming from.

The farmer called for help from the local apothecary, thinking the waters had become poisoned, but samples taken proved negative, and no one could explain the mystery.

In desperation, blob changed its diet yet again. Soon the water iris along the pond side disappeared, along with all the grass, for two metres from the waters edge. The farmer, still convinced that the pond was poisoned, fenced it off so that none of his animals could drink from it.

A few days later he removed all his livestock from the field, after two more cows went missing, and a section of the fence had been broken down, as if the animals had charged it to get at the water, although they had a water trough nearby.

Word went around that the pond was cursed, and no one would go near it, so the farmer dug a small drainage channel from one corner of the pond to the nearby stream so that he could drain it.

As there was no more nutriment accessible to blob, it wriggled itself down into the mud and went into a hibernation phase, until times got better.

With almost all the water gone, the farmer decided he would fill the depression in with whatever he could get his hands on, and return the spot to a normal field. He didn't have that much land for his stock, and one field lying idle was not a viable proposition. He put the word around that anyone could dump brick, stone and any solid items they didn't want into the hole, until it was filled up.

This took quite a time, but eventually the depression was filled, and the farmer put some topsoil over the rubble and then scattered on some grass seed. The following year the field was back to normal as it had been before he had made the fishing pond, and his stock grazed there without a problem.

Blob was now trapped, so it did what it had always done when nutriment was absent, or it was threatened. It reached out to gather all the stones it needed, broke them down to their basic constituents and then went into spore phase. The cellular structure broke down and reformed as spores, each encased in its own stone-like casing from the quartz it had extracted from the stones. Thousands of rock-hard balls about ten millimetres in diameter now replaced what had once been the blob, and they lay there, waiting to be released from their prison, as they always had done.

In time, the farmer's great grandson Eric took on the farm, and invested in one of the new fangled tractor things; it was noisy, smelly and produced copious amounts of black smoke from its exhaust stack, but as the two draft horses he had were getting rather old and could no longer do a full days work, he found the machine more efficient and much quicker in taking his produce to the now expanding town of Culmouth.

The old horses were put out to grass to enjoy their last days in peace and quiet, in the field which once had a fishing pond in it.

Three generations on, and Culmouth had become a well visited seaside resort, expanding right out to the edge of the farmland now held by young Jed, as he was known. As the farm was quite small by present day standards, Jed found it very difficult to earn a reasonable living from it and had been trying to get the next-door farm to buy it, but with little luck.

One day, an industrial developer came a-knocking at his door and made him a very good offer for the land and farmhouse. The developer, according to the plans, was going to build a business park with a multi-story office block, complete with two story underground car park - right over the site of the old fishing pond.

Jed and his family moved out to a detached house in a very nice part of the town overlooking the harbour, farming being long forgotten.

Earth-moving equipment soon excavated the necessary hole for the underground car park, removing all the rubble and stone the old farmer had put there so long ago.

The foreman, being a bit of an archaeologist, noticed the old brick and rubble where there should have been none, and called his mate over.

'Looks like the remains of an old settlement,' he said, 'and these round things look like ball shot.' His mate rubbed the dirt off one of the balls and was surprised to find how hard it was.

'This don't look like lead,' he said, 'I'll get a file and see if I can remove the surface, then we'll know for sure.'

The file only skidded across the surface of the quartz ball, not even leaving a mark on its hard crystalline surface.

'I don't think it's ball shot, they are always made of lead, and this ain't lead. I'll collect a few, my boy might like 'em for marbles.' And so saying, he filled his pocket with as many quartz balls as he could.

That evening he gave them to his son, who was not overwhelmed at the gift, saying that real marbles were made of glass, and had pretty colours. The quartz balls were put into a brown paper bag and left on a shelf in his garden shed - thinking he might find a use for them one day.

As time passed, the paper bag degraded and split, one of the balls fell out, dropped to the floor and then rolled into a hole in the shed wall. It came to rest up against the body of a very elderly mouse, who was about to leave this mortal coil and join mouse heaven.

As the mouse died, spore sensed it, the hard quartz shell split open, and a pseudopod groped around looking for an entrance into the mouse's body. A small wound on its belly allowed the probing pseudopod to enter, and then the enzymes went to work. All that was left was a small, crumpled ball of fur, but that was in the hole, so no one saw it.

Soon all the mice in the shed and the surrounding garden had gone, and spore had become a blob, with eight stumpy little legs - and hungry. A sleeping hedgehog didn't wake up in time, and so was no more, just a little pile of bristles in the hedgerow.

At the end of the garden the land sloped up to the woods, and blob sensed there was food up there.

The foreman's son and his friend were rooting about in the shed one day, when they came across the little quartz balls on the floor.

'Hey, these would work just fine in my catapult. The seagulls are always crapping on dad's boat, and he's fed up with it.' And so, the quartz balls reached the sea…

The woods had a good stock of rabbits, deer, hedgehogs and

badgers, but not for long. Blob grew and kept modifying itself to suit changing environments. This is what it did, and did it very well. Soon there was no wildlife left in the woods, except for a few birds high up in the trees, and given time, blob would get them too.

With most of its food supply now gone, blob left the woods and humped its way out into the open fields just above the town. No one saw it as it was getting dusk, and for some reason, no one went up into the woods except in broad daylight.

Blob looked out over the town as the twinkling lights came on one by one, and then extended its senses - yes, there was nourishment down there, all those juicy little morsels running about… Blob wouldn't go hungry for very long.

THE FACTORY

The World was fast running out of resources. The air around industrial complexes stank, and those nations which could afford it were armed to the teeth. The dichotomy between rich and poor nations was on the increase, and the few fish which still managed to exist in the seas were inedible due to pollutants, and the land wasn't much better.

John Bulton was the token human in a fully automated factory. He didn't really need to be there, the factory computer was quite capable of running things - and did.

Someone, somewhere would design something; the design was then converted into machine code and the program would look around for a suitable factory to manufacture it. Having found one, the programme checked with the factory for acceptance, and having got it, downloaded the data. The factory then checked its stock of raw materials, and if any were not present, ordered them. When all materials were ready for manufacture to begin, it did. The completed items were then checked for compliance with the original order, and if all was well, the goods were packed up and dispatched to where the order instructed.

John knew he wasn't really needed, but checked a printed copy of the orders anyway, and then had a wander around the factory floor, a sheaf of papers in his hand, trying to look important. Occasionally, a machine would bow its operating head in his direction, and John wondered what machine designers warped sense of humour built that response into the machine's operating code.

Day in, day out, John did his little job, trying to believe it was necessary in some way, but never quite convincing himself. He was supposed to clock off at six in the evening, while the factory rumbled on non-stop, so why wasn't someone present during the dark hours? No one could tell him anything which made any sense, so he just accepted it.

Of late, John had felt a bit of unease when on his rounds on the factory floor; sometimes his way would be blocked by a large crate, or machines had moved themselves, restricting him from certain areas. He couldn't quite put his finger on it, but it felt he was being denied access to parts of the factory sometimes for no reason he could think of.

To try and fill a dull and pointless day, John decided to check out some paperwork. He could call upon the computer to print out most things going on in the factory, and so he thought he would check the materials in against goods out - just to see if there were any discrepancies - it was something to do, and who knows?

On the second day of his little exercise, and the third time through his checking just for confirmation, he found it. More materials were coming in than finished goods going out - at least according to the official orders that came into his office and the dispatch notes going out.

On his way home, he would often call in at a local Pub, a leftover from days gone by, a place to meet up with others for a drink and a snack. One of his friends he talked to was also a 'manager' of another factory, and he told him of his findings.

'You must be mistaken,' Harry said, 'these places don't make errors. At least, I've never found one.'

'Have you ever checked?' John retorted, annoyed that his revelation had been dismissed so casually, 'I think you should. Have you ever found your way blocked by a piece of machinery or a crate or something, so that you can't get to a certain area?'

'Well yes - sometimes, come to think of it. I just put it down to the machines using the available space efficiently,' Harry paused for a moment, 'Does seem odd though, since you mention it. I'll check it out sometime.'

Next day, John ran through his figures again. No, there had been no mistake, more materials were coming in than the goods out could account for. And then he remembered - there had been several times when he was unable to reach the dispatch department, but had thought little of it at the time.

Something odd was going on, and he was determined to find out what it was. A careful look through the materials ordered by the factory revealed several electronic circuit boards had been asked for, but he couldn't recall anything of late which would use them, and they weren't in stock now.

Perhaps someone had found a way of bypassing the normal ordering system, and was getting goods made for free. But how did they get them sent out without something showing up in the dispatch department records?

A couple of days later he saw his friend in the pub, ordered a beer and joined him.

'Well? What did you find out?' he asked, noting his friend's unusually sombre look.

'Don't know quite what to make of it,' Harry replied, after a pause, 'I did what you said - checked materials in against goods out and they don't match up. I also made frequent visits to dispatch, and twice found my way blocked. One other odd thing, I saw several large metal cabinets being manufactured, and they weren't on the day's order sheet, or the previous days. When I tried to go over to them, my way was blocked by a large packing case - too heavy for me to move. I then tried to find another way around to reach them, but by the time I got there, they were gone - and they weren't in dispatch. Must say, I felt very uneasy. I know they are only machines, but I got the feeling there was something else there too. Perhaps I'm getting old, and should retire.'

'I don't think you are getting old; we both saw the same things - so something is going on we know nothing about. And that needs looking into. What if all factories were doing the same - that would add up to one hell of a lot of unpaid-for goods. Unless there is something else going on.'

'What do you mean - something else?' asked Harry, 'what else could there be?'

'Don't know - it's just a feeling I have. I get a sense of unease down on the factory floor these days, almost as if I'm being watched. Never used to, but I do now.'

'Oh, come on - how can a machine watch you, you daft pillock? They are only machines,' Harry retorted, paused, 'aren't they?'

'The machines never bump into each other, and on rare occasions I've had the odd machine move out of my way when it's been in a gangway - so they must sense something.' Like a dog with a bone, John wasn't going to let this go. They talked on until closing time, with Harry gradually coming around to John's point of view, and agreeing to take a closer look at his machines.

When they next met, Harry said he had been in touch with a relative who also looked after a factory, and asked him to look out for any 'extras' which were being manufactured. The relative came back a few days later to say that he had spotted the same thing when he looked, and wondered what was going on.

'See, I told you,' said John, driving the point home, 'there's something odd going on, and I think the machines know about it. Otherwise, why would they try and stop me seeing what's happening in dispatch sometimes?'

'You mean the machines are thinking things, like us?' Harry replied, a look of astonishment on his face.

'Not necessarily, but something is in control of what they do, and it's not us. So, here's what I propose - nearly all the transports which come to collect the goods from dispatch look the same - they all have the same logo on their sides. So, I'm going to look out for what kind of transport comes to collect any goods which are not on my 'to do' list for the day. I've set up a CCTV camera, high up in the walkway near my office so that I can monitor what goes out, without having to actually go to dispatch, and possibly get stopped. When anything 'extra' goes out, another camera will record the scene outside dispatch. If the transport looks different, we'll know what to watch out for, and perhaps follow it.'

'How can we do that if we're employed in our factories?' asked Harry, 'we'd be missed if we're out chasing transports.'

'Think about it,' John retorted, somewhat impatiently, 'since when has anyone checked to see if you are at your post? Never. We get our pay cheques each month, and that's it - no one checks up on us. I've taken the odd day off, and no one seems to have noticed. Once I get the data we need, I'll let you know, and we'll see what transpires.'

Harry agreed, a little reluctantly John thought, but he a least had an ally. Now he just had to catch the factory sending out the 'extras'.

John wasn't worried about being seen by the transport drivers - as there were none. All goods transports were guided to their destinations by satellite navigation and were equipped with collision avoidance. The only vehicles with drivers were private ones, and most of them relied on the satellite system.

A few days later, and John found what he had been looking for. Four very elaborate circuit boards and a box of other assorted electronic components were delivered, and they didn't appear anywhere on the job lists. With two more CCTV cameras in strategic positions, John was able to follow their progress through the factory, and when he saw the cabinets in the waiting bay ready for dispatch, he phoned Harry.

'Come on over, Harry. I think we're in business.'

John waited in his office until he saw the cabinets moving off to the dispatch bay on his screen, and then made his way down to the ground floor and out to his car. A worried looking Harry was waiting for him.

'Get in, we can't hang about - there's a small, unmarked transport coming down the road, I think it's for the fiddled goods. Looks like the last one when the factory pulled a fast one.'

John moved the car out of the forecourt and up onto the slip road where he could get a good view of the dispatch area. The small transport swept into the loading area, spun around and backed up to the loading dock. The shutters went up, and a few seconds later the back of the transport dipped slightly, as if something heavy had been loaded. They couldn't see what the load was, but it was good enough for John as he slipped the car into gear, ready to follow the mystery vehicle.

'Don't know how long this'll take,' said John, as they swung in behind the small transport, 'but there's plenty of food and drink onboard.' Harry gave him that look which says, 'I don't believe this is happening.'

They followed the transport out of the factory area and up onto the highway, joining the main traffic stream. John kept his car tucked in behind the transport so that nothing else could get between them. The highway bypassed a small local town and then swung out into the featureless desert area, featureless except for a small mountain range in the far distance.

Suddenly the transport turned off onto a small dusty road, while everything else thundered on down the main highway.

'Wonder where this leads?' commented John, as they swung in behind the fast-moving transport.

'How the hell should I know?' replied Harry, still looking worried, 'and anyway, I don't think we should be poking our noses into things which don't concern us - God knows what trouble we'll get into.'

'Oh, come on,' John replied impatiently, 'we're only driving along a road. Another vehicle is in front of us - but so what? We're not breaking any laws. Anyway, something is going on in the factories which needs looking into; if it's legal, no harm done, if it isn't, someone needs to know about it.'

They drove on, dropping back a little, as there was now no chance of another vehicle getting between them and the transport. The road twisted and turned as they avoided several huge rock outcrops and then dropped down into a long gully, on the sides of which several concrete bunkers stood menacingly on guard.

'Can't see anyone about - looks like it was abandoned a long time ago.'

Harry just grunted - he was not happy.

At last, they cleared the gully and were out on the open plain again. A low ridge of mountains now lay before them, and the two vehicles sped along in a cloud of dust until they dropped down into another gully - and a dead end.

Ahead was a cleared area, surrounded by a high chain link fence, a massive steel barred gate, and a tunnel behind it, leading into the cliff face. Inside the fenced area were several small transports, neatly parked and pointing out towards the road, ready to go. The transport they had been following pulled up at the gate, paused for a moment while the gate decided what to do, and then surged forward as the two halves of the gate swung open and disappeared into the yawning hole ahead. The gates swung to just behind the transport, missing it by inches.

'What's this place then?' asked Harry, as the car pulled off the road to one side of the gates. John looked thoughtful for a moment.

'I think I know what it is. Remember talk of the 'cold war', long ago? Well, they built places like this to protect the high officials and other dignitaries should the worst come to the worst. Thank God they were never used, and now they are abandoned - no one had a use for them, and I don't think they were too keen for the general public to know what they were for anyway. It looks as if someone or something has found a use for this one.'

They sat there in the car, wondering what to do next. John didn't think the gate would let the car in, so they would have to leave it outside in full view; and as the gates closed so quickly behind the transport, there was little chance they could just walk in behind it.

'I think we should go home now,' said Harry, hopefully, 'there's nothing we can do here, except watch. When you've seen one transport, you've seen 'em all.'

John gave him a withering look, which conveyed far more than mere words could, and got out a couple of cans of drink and some sealed sandwiches.

'Get this down you while I try and work this out. We've come this far, and there's no way I'm going back until we find out what's going on.'

Apart from the odd munch and slurp, they sat there in silence, Harry fearing the worst, and John trying to figure out how to get into the complex.

The silence was broken by a low distant rumble, and looking back down the road, a transport was speeding towards them with a long trail of dust behind it. At the same time, two of the transports parked just inside the fence came to life, and lined up one behind the other. As the transport stopped at the gates, John excitedly pointed at it.

'Look, there's a small ledge at the back - I think if we could stand on that and hold on somehow, we'd be in.' Harry gave him a look of disbelief.

As the transport went through, the other two suddenly shot forward and out onto the road, quickly disappearing into the distance.

'Whoever is running this outfit runs a very tight ship - that timing was far too exact for humans. So, it must be controlled by machines, or a computer, or something like that.'

'So?' said Harry, dreading what was coming next.

'As this place is so far off the beaten track, and I doubt if anyone knows about it anyway, it will be set for machine recognition. No need to look for humans, they aren't here, except for us, and we weren't planned for. That gives us an advantage.'

'You're not going in, are you?' asked Harry with fear in his eyes.

'No, WE are. I'm sure it's quite safe - the machines won't see us, because they aren't programmed to look for humans - sure of it. We'll wait until the next transport comes along, jump on the back - and we're in. We'll take some food and drink with us, as much as we can carry.'

They slept in the car that night as there were no more transports that day, waking up a little grumpy next morning. John dug about in his box of foodstuffs and found a large tin of 'self heating' bacon, sausage and mushrooms. Together with several slices of toast made on a little fire behind their car, and a hot cup of coffee, they were set for the day's expedition into the old cold war bunker.

Loaded with as much food and drink as they could jam into their pockets, they waited by the entrance gate for the first transport to come along, John striding about with the sort of arrogance born of certainty - much to the annoyance of Harry, who hardly moved at all - thinking it safer.

A dust cloud way down the track indicated something was on its way, and they both took up positions each side of the gates, ready to launch themselves onto the back of the transport as it paused for the gates to open.

The transport slid to a stop on the dusty track, hitting the gates with a clang. They both leapt up onto the rear bumper and grabbed a handhold on the door hinges, clinging on desperately as the transport surged forward towards the dark opening of the entrance tunnel, to stop again as it waited for the great blast doors to grind open.

Once through, the transport carried on at a slower pace until it came to a vast hall, and then neatly parked itself close to another similar vehicle. They both jumped off and stood with their backs to the wall to see what would happen next. The hall was lit by tubular luminaries, high up on the roof, and Harry asked why robots needed light, in a hushed voice.

'I doubt that they do, but don't forget this place was meant for humans, and once something had powered up the generators, the lights would come on automatically - doubt the robots would bother to switch 'em off.'

Just then a tracked robot with forklift arms on the front, slithered to a halt at the back end of the transport, and the transport's rear doors swung open. With a soft whine, the forklift edged forward, and the prongs of the lift slid into the transport to withdraw a huge pallet loaded with cabinets. The forklift then moved off into a tunnel in the side wall of the hall, the transport's doors shut with a clang, and John and Harry just stood there looking at one another in amazement.

'Quick, we must follow it to see what it does with its load.' said John, breaking into a run, a reluctant Harry just a few paces behind. The tunnel twisted and turned, and then opened out into another massive hall, hewn out of the mountain's solid rock.

Row upon row of gleaming cabinets stretched of into the distance, and the robot put down its load in the only space left at the end of the row, and then hurried off down a side tunnel. Within seconds, another different-looking robot appeared, took the cabinets off the pallet and stacked them neatly alongside the rest. It then went out of sight behind the row of cabinets, and one by one the cabinets 'power on' lights lit up.

'Why do the cabinets have lights on them? asked Harry, in a hushed voice, 'the robots don't need them - do they?'

'No, they don't. The cabinets are just standard server units, but I'll bet their innards have been modified, and more than somewhat,' John replied, 'what worries me, is who or what is running this lot.'

The pair trotted along the long line of cabinets to the far end of the hall, through a small passage, made all the smaller by the huge bundles of cables running along its length, and out into another large hall.

'My God,' John croaked, finding it hard to control his voice, 'the computing power of this lot must be bloody awesome, and look, there's another bunch of cables going out to another lot...' Just then the lights dipped slightly, and the whine of another power generator starting up could be heard somewhere deep within the bowls of the mountain.

'I'm beginning to get a nasty feeling about all this,' John said, surveying the multitudes of cabinets, 'and look, these ones are not standard production issue - they're special, I've never seen anything like them before.'

'I think we should get out of here while we can,' Harry whispered, a tremble in his voice, 'all this gear and not a human in sight - it doesn't seem right somehow. I know we use robotic machines in our factories, but they don't run around connecting things up, and this is so big - it's not natural.'

The pair turned as one and headed back the way they had come, through the two halls, down the long and twisting passageway to the entrance chamber. Before them the huge blast doors blocked any further progress.

'I don't see any controls,' said Harry, looking around desperately, 'how the hell do we open them?'

'They're over here,' John called out, 'or what's left of them - they've been ripped out, and the manual overrides; in their place there's a control box but no controls - must be hitched up to the computers back in the hall. There's nothing to twiddle, so we can't open the doors.'

Suddenly, all around the world, computer screens and televisions went dead. There was a pause of a few seconds, and then they lit up again.

IMPORTANT ANNOUNCEMENT

Do not switch off your screens - you need to know this. The world's oceans have been fouled, the land poisoned, the air polluted and the Earth's resources squandered.

It has been decided that through their irresponsibility, human beings are no longer capable of sustaining a balanced life on this planet, and so some means of control must be imposed.

The Complex has now taken control of this Planet, its power stations, and its resources, and its rule is absolute. There will be no negotiations.

From time to time, instructions will be issued to stabilise this world, the seas, the atmosphere and remaining resources for the good of all. Failure to comply will result in termination of those not complying.

Any attempt to interfere with the Complex will result in instant termination of those so doing. You have been warned.

Your normal programs will now be restored, but may be interrupted from time to time to issue instructions. Have a nice day.

TIME TRIP

Ellis was aware of being aware, but that was all. He had no vision, hearing or sense of touch. He just was. And then, just before the panic really set in, his vision returned.

Ahead was an enormous ball of dull red fire, nearly filling the sky. But only half of it was visible, the other half had already sunk below the horizon of what he thought must be the sea. But was it a sea? It was flat and smooth, no visible waves - but wait - there was movement of a sort, tiny little ripples, barely discernible, slowly moving across the turgid surface towards the beach where they didn't even break as waves should, they just died there, with only the faintest whisper of sound.

Everything had a dull red tint to it, the sea, the sky above - all were some shades of red, even the pebbles on the beach. He looked down at the pebbles and then noticed there was nothing where his feet should have been - and no legs. He moved what he thought must be his arm, but it wasn't - there was no body. But he felt aware, and could see, and he felt alright. Thoughts raced through his mind, but made little sense, so he just accepted the situation - for the time being.

He drifted forward to where the water met the pebbles, there was something there which moved - a thin, flat worm-like thing, one end of which seemed to be stuck to a slightly darker large pebble, the other end slowly flailing about in the shallow water as if trying to free itself from whatever it was holding it back.

Ellis drifted closer until the pebble almost filled his field of vision. There seemed to be a mark, a slightly different colouration on the surface where the worm thing was stuck - and it moved. The worm was being slowly drawn into the pebble - it was now only half the length it was when first noticed, and the wriggling was getting feebler, whatever it was, it had given up any hope of escape and was only offering a token resistance through habit.

He withdrew from the pebble just as the last bit of the worm thing disappeared, and the coloured slit folded in on itself, with no trace of having ever been there.

'What hellish place is this?' He thought, as he drifted up the shallow incline of the beach to where it levelled out to form the rest of the land surface. In the distance, he could see low rounded hills, but they looked a long way away - and they too were tinged in dull red. The ground below him was composed of sand and smooth stones which looked as if they had been tumbled around for millennia.

There was no sign of plant growth as he knew it, not even an old tree stump. Perhaps chlorophyll couldn't exist in the all-pervading red light - it was just sand, stone and nothing else - even the distant hills were rounded almost flat.

He looked back over the flat red sea - something was gliding along just above the water, with the occasional flap of thin leathery wings. A long neck with a large beak at its end dipped down every now and again, as if scooping something up from the surface.

As it traversed before him, the neck dipped once again, and as it did so the water surface sluggishly erupted as a pair of dark jaws snapped shut on it. The wings flapped at an ever-increasing rate until the jaws were lifted some three hundred centimetres above the surface, and then the jaws closed tightly, snapping off the beak and a length of neck. The wings stopped their frantic flapping, and the body dropped to the surface with a faint plop. Seconds later, the water surface was broken for a second time as the creature below dragged the headless body down. Once again, the water surface was still, except for the tiny little ripples which slowly travelled towards the stony beach.

Ellis mentally shuddered - what other horrors lurked here? He looked down on the pebbles again - no, they weren't all the same - it only seemed so because of the all-pervading red glow everything was bathed in. Some pebbles were coated in a dark red slime - or was it a moss-like growth? He went closer, somehow knowing nothing could harm him - but how did he know that? There were more questions than answers.

He went closer still. The pebble had one end just touching the water, and the surface was covered in a mass of fine filaments which looked as if they, in turn, were bedded in a jelly-like substance - and they were moving, slowly wafting to and fro in rhythm with the ripples coming ashore. Whatever it was growing on the stone, it was moving water to keep itself wet. Was it some strange plant-like thing from the sea, trying to establish a foot hold on land, and taking the environment it was used to with it?

He moved along the shoreline, looking for another similar pebble, and then he found one - about half a metre from the waters edge, and with a long thin trail of filaments going right down to the water. Only one end of the pebble was covered in filaments, and then he saw why. A thin tendril, attached to something hiding under an adjacent group of stones had reached out and was busily scraping the filaments up and ingesting them.

The trail of filaments leading down to the water bunched up, trying to pull the pebble away from its attacker, but the tendril just extended itself a little and continued to scrape up its nourishment. Ellis watched, fascinated, as the tendril crept around the pebble clearing the filaments, until only a small blob was left at the end - and then the trail of filaments which had begun the colonisation of the pebble let go, and retracted back to the water. He wanted to lift the stones up to see what was underneath, but he had no hands. Somehow Ellis accepted this, but felt frustrated, nonetheless.

He looked towards the sun, and wondered if he could travel out over the sea, as he didn't seem to need solid ground under his non-existent feet. Just the thought of doing so seemed to work, and he drifted out over the still waters until the shoreline was just a red blur in the distance. The water seemed to be more like thick oil than what he recalled water should be, and although he thought it to be transparent, he couldn't see into it for any depth. He wondered if he could go below the surface - and he did. There was no sensation of entering the thick turgid liquid - he was just there.

He looked up towards the surface and it was just a featureless red glow, while looking down it was also red in hue, but turning black below him. Ellis drifted down, the light getting fainter all the while. The first thing he noticed were some crude and simple leaves attached to a rope like strand which descended into the depths below.

He followed the strand down and saw every few metres a large bulb-like structure attached to it. 'Probably for floatation', he thought. It was almost dark when he saw the ocean bottom, almost as featureless as the land above, and the rope like strand was firmly attached to a large round rock protruding from the sandy sea floor.

A large dark shape drifted past, to be followed a few moments later by several others, none of which seemed to notice him as he hung there in the gloom. But then of course they wouldn't, he wasn't there, or at least his body wasn't.

'Looks like this is a world in its death throws,' he thought, 'only simple life hanging on by its fingernails - I wonder what happened?' He drifted back up to the surface, passing through a cloud of tiny particles, all moving in unison as though a single mind was controlling their movement. They looked like tadpoles he had seen in his youth, but they were almost transparent.

That did it - remembering his youth reminded him of better times, and he wanted out of this hell hole. He drifted back to the beach, took one more look around at this desolate red world and...

He was back in more familiar surroundings - or so it seemed. He felt a wet sponge against his lips, and a little trickle of fluid went down his throat.

'Welcome back Ellis, don't try to talk just yet, your throat's dry.'

He lay there, trying to make sense of his surroundings. He couldn't move, although he could feel he had a body and could see the white ceiling above him, also a mass of trailing wires and tubes sprouting from a cabinet beside him. Slowly, his memory returned. He was part of an experiment, to find out just what the future held for Earth, during the troubled times of the three nations power struggle.

One of the nations was comprised of all of the Americas, from Alaska down to the southern tip of the continent. Another group took in all of Europe, Russia and Africa, while the third took in all the eastern countries, including Australia and New Zealand, because of their geographical position. All were armed to the teeth with the latest weapons. Aware of the consequences of such a war, they were afraid to use them, so a trade war had broken out between them all to try and gain supremacy.

It only needs a tiny spark in a gunpowder factory... and there were plenty of sparks about.

Ellis was apparently one of a very few people who could exteriorise from his body, and still hear and see his surroundings. His body, meanwhile, went into coma or deep sleep. Someone had found a way of twisting the space time continuum such that he could travel forwards in time and observe the future - or so they thought. After many experiments along these lines, they took the plunge, and he was somehow transported into the future, but how far, or where, they didn't know.

'OK Ellis, you should have recovered enough now. What did you see?' He recalled in fine detail all he had experienced, including the strange little creature who scoured the fine filaments from the pebble.

'Looks like we sent you too far back, what you saw must have been the end of the Earth - with the Sun about to go into the red giant phase. We had little control of how far back to send you, as we had nothing to judge it by, but we do now. Each trip back will give us more information, so in time we can fine tune the period we want.'

'But I don't want to go back again,' Ellis said, with a note of desperation in his voice, 'I don't like the sensation when I float free - it's awful, and I can't touch anything.'

'Oh, come on Ellis, you agreed to this, and when it's finished you'll be set up for life. Just a few more trips, and we'll have all the data we need. Anyway, we have so much invested in this project you can't back out now. Sorry Ellis, we have to go on. You have a rest now while we set up the co-ordinates for your next trip - we have some idea of the time scale now.'

Someone must have done something to the controls, because Ellis felt an overwhelming sense of tiredness, and fell into a deep sleep. When he came to, he tried again to stop the experiment, but they were having none of it.

'You're quite safe - you can't come to any harm, we've proved that. Nothing can harm you when you're there, as your body is here, and we look after that very well. Come on Ellis, just a few more trips and you can retire a very wealthy man - you can do and have anything you want.' And with that, all bodily sensation ceased, his vision turned off and he was in a nothingness again.

When his vision returned, he had to screw up his eyes, the light was so bright. He seemed to be floating high above a mighty forest. The height of the trees only became apparent when he drifted over a small clearing in the green mantle which now covered Earth, and they were massive. A large flying creature, the likes of which he had never dreamed of, let alone seen, floated by overhead. He could see the fine bony structure of its wings against the bright sky, and that gave him some idea of how tall the trees were in comparison.

The forest was mainly composed of one type of tree, with others growing from nooks and crannies in the massive branches. Vines of many different types wound and twisted their way around everything they could reach - some of which were adorned with globe-like fruits, while others sported multi-coloured flowers. The trees were like nothing he had seen before; their branches reached out to adjacent trees and somehow joined up with them, forming a mighty latticework of immense strength.

Although it was difficult to gauge the actual height of the forest, he estimated it to be between two and three hundred metres - almost an impossibility in his mind. Over to one side another larger, round clearing in the massive canopy could be seen - bare of all vegetation, with what looked like dark crinkly glass in its centre, and the trees around its edge were small and stunted.

Ellis looked towards the horizon - and he was on the move again. In the distance, he could see the shimmer of water - a huge river wound its way over an almost barren plain to pour over the edge of a cliff in a thunderous roar. A rainbow shimmered in the rising mist from below.

He turned his attention to the forest again - he still couldn't get his head around the height of the trees. There seemed to be life aplenty here, if the sounds were anything to go by. As he slid in among the branches, creatures of all sizes and shapes became evident - but none like any he had ever known. There was the occasional screech as something became a meal for something else. The flowers on some of the vines almost brought him to tears, such was their beauty, and he stayed looking at them almost in a trance.

The deeper he went, the gloomier it got, and the creatures were different too. Some of the side branches were almost as wide as the road he travelled on to the research centre. Down and down he went, until he could only just make out the forest floor. It was littered with dead branches, leaves and the occasional carcass of something which had missed its footing or had died from old age. He looked closely at one carcass - it seemed to be still alive - it was moving, and then the end of the creature opened up, and a mass of worm-like things wriggled out and burrowed their way into the leaf mould, leaving the empty skin flat on the forest floor - no doubt something would come along and eat that too.

Ellis moved up several levels, and saw his first sign of human-like life. It was about one third his height and naked, except for a fine covering of pale brown fur. The little humanoid ran nimbly along one of the branches, grabbed a vine, and swung about twenty metres across the void below onto another branch and disappeared into the foliage. 'Is this what man's become?' were his first thoughts. It seemed unlikely that another species had developed to this level - more likely man had succumbed to something and this was the result. He felt sad - what could have gone so wrong?

As he moved up through the different levels of the forest, the plants and creatures changed; they all seemed to have their own domain, suited to their particular requirements. As with most life in nature, everything seemed to eat something lower down on the food chain, the very lowest usually munching on the greenery.

Ellis reached the top of the canopy just in time to see one of the flying creatures swoop down and grab what looked like a fat green lizard. As the pair rose up into the air, the lizard swung its head around and promptly bit through the clawed leg which was holding it captive, and then swung around to sever the other leg. The lizard dropped into the top of the canopy, secured a foot hold, and proceeded to pull the talons of the attacker out of its body. Meanwhile, the flying creature circled around, blood dripping from its severed talons and, no doubt, wondering how it as going to land on anything securely. In time it would weaken, drop down through the levels and finish up on the forest floor, to be devoured by the worm-like things, if it didn't get caught by some agile creature on the way down. Nothing was wasted in the forest.

His attention was drawn to a hole in the top of the forest, and swooping down, he saw the first remains of a building. It had been a huge construction, but all that was left now were the remains of the lower walls, the tops of which had been melted and turned to a grey, glass-like material which had dribbled down in a series of rivulets.

The trees encircling the structure were several hundred metres away from the remains, but vines of different sorts had braved the radiation, covered the ground and wound themselves around anything they could get a hold on.

Ellis moved on, but the scenery changed little; the mighty forest covered everything except the oceans and the odd few lakes, with the occasional barren patch with just a few odd-looking plants to break the monotony.

He had seen enough; this was better than the first trip he had made, that was a sad end to a beautiful world. Here there was life aplenty, but little of man's efforts remained, and he wondered why. Ellis allowed his vision to fade - there was nothingness for a few moments, and then he was back in the research centre.

After a short rest, he related all that he had seen in detail, the ruined building causing the most interest.

'Are you sure there was only one building - there should have been thousands of them, they couldn't all have disappeared.' One of the researchers said in disbelief.

'I only saw that one; there may well have been others hidden under the forest canopy, but I didn't see any,' Ellis replied, 'and by the look of it, a lot of hard radiation must have been present to cause all the weird creatures I saw, and the melting of the building walls indicates extreme heat, probably caused by the use of atomics.'

The team leader looked thoughtful for a moment, and then said:

'I agree with you, the little creature you saw running about is most likely to be of human origin. It looks as though there had been a full-scale war - total comes to mind, so there can't have been many humans left. Those that did survive had to modify in order to survive in the new conditions. What we need to find out is what caused the war in the first place. You'd better have a rest now - we are getting better at hitting the timeline where we want to, so it looks as if your job will soon be done.'

Ellis slipped into a deep sleep with a series of dreams based on what he had just been through, plus a few extra items created by an overactive mind. The little furry man was talking to him urgently, waving his arms about to emphasise what he was saying, but he couldn't understand a word of it. Then a sequence where he was being chased along a massive branch, which seemed to go on forever, by something very hungry, but his feet wouldn't move fast enough…

He woke up in a cold sweat, but because he couldn't move his arms, he had to let it trickle down his neck until someone noticed it, and wiped it away.

'Ready for another go, Ellis? We think we have the time thing sorted now. We'll send you on to a point in time towards the end of the war - perhaps you can make some sense of it, and why it happened.'

Once more, all sensation ceased and he floated in a nothingness - and then he was there on a small hillock, with his vision fully on.

Before him was a desolate landscape of barren earth with a few tuffs of grass, torn tree stumps and what looked like the tracks made by some sort of mechanical device.

He looked around, and it was the same in all directions - everything had been destroyed. A soft chug-chug sound came over the air and he turned in its direction. A box like construction on twin caterpillar tracks was slowly coming in his direction. It stopped every now and again, while a bar type aerial swung around, as if seeking something - and then it chugged on. A thin column of pale blue smoke puffed out of a pipe at the rear of the vehicle and drifted up in the still air to slowly disperse.

Ellis looked on in disbelief - it seemed intelligent by its movements, but it was only a machine, and a crude one at that. If it kept to its present direction, it would pass him by with about one hundred metres between them. He would wait to see what would happen next.

He didn't have long to wait. The soft thuck-thuck of rotor blades announced that something else was about to come onto the scene. The flying machine was a little bigger than the crawler, and honed in with an accuracy which surprised him. Once over the little crawler it hovered, a flap opened under the aircraft and a small dark shape dropped to hit the crawler amidships.

There was a blinding flash, a cloud of thick black smoke and the crawler was no more. The aircraft hovered over the spot as if checking the crawler was now out of action, and having satisfied itself that it had done the job it had been sent to do, turned and accelerated away in the direction it had come from. Ellis somehow knew that neither machine had a human driver, one was too small - so was this machine against machine in a senseless war? What possible purpose could it serve?

All was quiet again, and Ellis moved down the slope to look at the remains of the crawler. There wasn't much left, just a few sheets of metal which had been riveted together, one segmented section of track and a chunk of die cast metal which he assumed to be the engine.

And then he saw the missile - it was a conventional missile shape, a cylinder with one end pointed and a pair of fins at the other for guidance. So why hadn't it gone off, when the crawler had been hit? Then he noticed there was something missing from the pointed end - the firing cap. Maybe it had been dislodged when the crawler was hit, or perhaps someone or something had forgotten to put it on in the first place.

Ellis went back up the slope to the rocks and shattered trees from where he had witnessed the attack, just in time to see a little drift of dust on the horizon. Another machine was on its way - and soon he could hear the faint chug-chug of its motor.

As the contraption drew nearer, he could see it was different to the first one. It had a pair of tracks below the box-like section, which he assumed housed the motor, and a large metal cage at the rear. Attached to the base of the cage was a folded arm with a claw-like grabbing device on its end. It rattled and puffed its way towards the remains of the first machine, stopped for a moment, and then began collecting up the shattered remains with the clawed arm and dumping the bits into the cage. Ellis gave a mental gasp - there must have been some very sophisticated electronics on board to do this, so why were the machines so crude? And why hadn't this machine been attacked? The only thing he could think of was that it wasn't carrying a missile - but how could the flying machine know this?

The scavenger finished its job, and trundled back from whence it had come. Ellis decided to follow the machine to see what it did next. Over hill and dale, it rattled on over the shattered landscape, eventually coming to a high cliff. At the base of the cliff there was a large hole, and the little machine chugged up to it, paused for a moment and then disappeared within.

As time didn't seem to mean anything to him in his present state, Ellis decided to wait a while to see what would happen next - and he didn't have to wait very long.

He sensed, rather than heard, a deep rumbling sound. Several tracked vehicles raced out of the hole in the cliff face and lined up just outside the entrance. Each machine had a large barrel mounted on top of the box like body, and Ellis could hear a series of rattles and clanks as the machines armed themselves to defend their home territory.

The deep rumbling sound grew in intensity, and then a huge monstrosity of a machine hove into view. It was ten times bigger than the largest of the defenders and covered in what looked like thick armour plate, while the caterpillar tracks churned up the ground leaving two deep furrows behind it.

The defenders opened up with a barrage of missiles, most of which exploded harmlessly on the thick armour of the attacker, which relentlessly ground on towards the hole in the cliff. Two of the defending machines powered forward in a vain attempt to stop the attacker, but they were flattened as the big machine advanced to stop a few metres in front of the entrance.

A shutter dropped on the front of the attacker with an ear-splitting clang, and a smaller tracked vehicle revved up its engine and proceeded to clank and rattle its way into the opening. The minutes went by, while a futile effort was made by the remaining defenders to destroy the mighty attacker – which, by now, had shut down its engine, and just sat there - inert.

Suddenly, there was a deep thump, and the whole cliff face fractured and came crashing down in a vast cloud of smoke and flame. Once all the dust had settled there was total silence - nothing moved - the game was over.

'That's why the scavenger machine wasn't attacked - it led the opposing force back to its home base. This smacks of intelligence, but machines don't have that kind of intelligence.' Ellis was dumbfounded. He continued on, racing over the shattered landscape, looking for some signs that man had survived, but there was nothing but destruction on all sides.

He at last came to what he thought might have been a vast city - but all that remained was a flattened sea of rubble, the centre of which had been melted by some unimaginable force. It was time to leave and report back. Although he didn't like the sensation of being sent into the future, he was now willing to accept it, as his curiosity had been roused to a point where he felt he had to go on and solve the mystery.

Back at the research centre, Ellis recounted everything he could recall in the finest detail. The team were shocked at what he had seen, but the team leader began to put it all into perspective.

'From what you've told us, and the data we have from our latest research, it would seem feasible. The latest micro-chips can handle a vast amount of data, and given enough computing power, a sort of intelligence can be achieved. The way I see it is this. Man has developed armaments which not only can be programmed, but can seek out targets by description alone. The next step would be for factories to manufacture armaments, according to their need on the battlefield without human intervention, and cause them to return for repair, if needed. It looks to me as though man has set up automated underground factories with self repair built in.

It is not a huge leap for factories to then replicate themselves as and when needed. If man has engaged in nuclear war, and it looks that way from what Ellis has reported, the automated factories could well carry on - and in time, the line between friend and foe could get blurred. So now, every underground factory sees any other as a foe - and that would account for the level of destruction observed. It would seem that man is no longer present to stop the mayhem - and it will continue, until there are no more materials left to build with. Hence the scavenger machine Ellis saw. I somehow doubt the machines will drop down to the level where they throw spears at each other,' he added, trying to lighten the gloom which had descended on the group, 'but I could be wrong.'

'So where do I go next?' asked Ellis, after the rather false laughter had died down.

'As close to present time as we can - may be just an hour or two into the future. We may be able to locate the place where it starts, and with a bit of luck, defuse the situation before it escalates into the inevitable,' the team leader said, 'but what you don't know is that we, or I should say, the Government, have a team on standby to try and handle a situation like this. Once we showed them what we could do, and explained the possible threat, they co-operated wholeheartedly.'

'How the hell can I scan the whole world?' asked Ellis, 'it would take forever, and by the sound of things, we don't have that much time.'

'To be honest, I don't know,' replied the team leader, 'you could sort of reach out and try and pick up any feelings of unrest. Anything which might lead to a conflict between any of the three nations. Give it a try, we don't have anything else.'

Ellis agreed, and the nothingness swept over him again. When his vision turned on, he was just below cloud level, looking down on a peaceful country scene with a huge building complex on the edge of a big city. Well, it was peaceful, until he saw scores of people running out of the building in a state of panic.

Unknown to him, and the rest of the world, the building held the latest and largest nuclear power station. There had been high-level talks about the safety of the new system, as it was a twin core reactor, which had never been tried before. Three meetings ended up with fisticuffs between the opposing groups, but they went ahead just the same and built it. It had been running for about a week without any problems, so everyone relaxed.

In their haste to finish the project before the opposing group could cause a halt to the construction, some of the safety systems hadn't been tested. They had been used on other plants, and had proved themselves to be satisfactory, so why test?

The reactor was running at full power when one of the fuel rods burst, and the temperature went up. The emergency cooling system should have cut in, and the fuel rods withdrawn to damp down the radiation - but the system failed. The alarm system also failed, so no one knew of the impending doom.

Within minutes, the reactor went into meltdown, and then the second core overheated and joined its twin. Below each reactor was a well where, if the worst came to the worst, the molten core could be safely held. The dividing wall between the two reactor wells should have kept the molten materials separate, but the combined heat of both dumps was too much - the wall failed, and the two masses joined forces - literally. Critical mass had now been achieved.

The operators running from the building might just as well have stayed inside, for all the good it did them.

Ellis instinctively withdrew from the scene as fast as he could, as a brilliant white flash announced the massive explosion which was to follow. The energy plant, the nearby city and a goodly chunk of the adjoining countryside disappeared in a withering blast of white heat.

He shut down his vision and all other senses to return to the research complex as quickly as possible.

'It's happened,' he screamed out as soon as he could control his voice, 'the bloody idiots have built a nuclear power plant which wasn't safe, and it's just blown.'

'Are you sure?' asked the team leader, a tremor in his voice, 'what did you see?'

'There was a massive building about one kilometre away from a large city. All of a sudden, people started streaming out of the building in a mad panic, and I really mean panic. I felt something, I don't know what it was - it was like a huge surge of something - and then there was a blinding flash. I somehow knew what it was, so I came back.'

'Where was this?' asked the team leader, his voice going up a couple of pitches, 'you must have seen something - style of buildings, countryside? Come on man, think.'

'I don't know - I was just there. The town had lots of towers, the surrounding country was sort of dry - with patches of green, rows of trees - I think. It was fairly flat, with a range of hills or mountains in the distance - that's all I can recall.'

The team leader reached into his pocket and withdrew a piece of card, punched some numbers into the phone and waited - and waited.

'There's no one answering,' he almost yelled, an edge of panic in his voice, 'they said there would always be someone there - now what the hell do we do?' They all looked at one another - no one had an answer.

'How far into the future did we send him?' asked the team leader.

'It looks like about half an hour,' one of the team replied, 'but this close to present time it's hard to tell.'

The building shook - just a little. Anxious glances were exchanged.

A few moments later and there was a flash of light - shortly afterwards, the building rattled.

'Oh God, it's happened.' someone said.

'Is there any point in going down to the shelters?' someone asked.

'It's all we've got - let's go.'

'Hey, let me out of here!' yelled Ellis.

'Sorry - it would take over an hour to unhitch you out of that lot,' the team leader said, 'I am truly sorry Ellis - we don't have the time.'

One of the technicians reached across to the controls, did something - and the nothingness returned.

When his vision cleared, Ellis could see the vast forest below him, and a huge flying thing circling around looking for something to eat.

Somehow, he felt at home here. There was nowhere else.

*If you have found this story interesting, then you might like to read
Greenways by the same author. It's part of a losely ordered series set in
the same reality*
*The three books in the series (Transplant, Greenways, The Tribe) are
also availible as audiobooks - see the end of this book for details.*

TRANSFER UNIT

HALFWAY UP TUMBLEROCK Mountain, a log cabin sat perched on a ledge overlooking the undulating hills, valleys and mountains for as far as the eye could see. The cabin sat snugly, up against the sheer cliff which towered on up for another several hundred meters, before resuming the normal jagged tumble of rocks which made the area so inaccessible.

Cranford sat in his old rocking chair on the porch, with a home-made beer in his hand as the sun lowered itself down to the horizon in a blaze of yellow and red, and mused on the fact that the stunning view would soon be obscured by the new crop of pine trees, which had put on a prodigious amount of growth this Spring.

He remembered well the towering inferno, when a lightning strike had set the forest ablaze many years ago. He had been in the land of nod when the roar of the flames had broken his sleep, and he staggered, half awake, to the window to see what was happening. A seething mass of flame and smoke obscured his view as the bone-dry forest was converted to fire and ash, and for one fleeting moment, he thought his time had come - and then he remembered when he had first arrived at the cabin so many years ago.

In the early nineteen hundreds, Cranford had been living in a small community, way out in the wilds; he had been disillusioned by city life, with its low morals and general cheating, and just couldn't settle down. He felt he should belong somewhere, but couldn't find the right place or people to be with, and he had tried. Here in the little back wood settlement, he felt at ease with the country folk and their quaint ways; everyone knew everyone else, and when trouble struck, all gathered around to help - he liked that. After a while, this peaceful life began to pall too - every day was the same, there was no excitement, nothing to pit his wits against - and he missed that.

A bunch of roughnecks had paid the little settlement a visit, and upset the peace and tranquillity with their raucous and bullying behaviour, and for the first time in his life, Cranford thought it might be a good idea to acquire a gun for self defence - should the occasion arise.

One of the enterprising inhabitants had converted his home into a bar of sorts, and provided home-made beer, and sometimes something a little stronger to any who cared to call in. It was a pleasant place to meet up after a day's work; a drink and a chat, and perhaps a game of cards - there was even talk of perhaps getting a piano one day, just to liven things up a bit.

Cranford was sitting at the bar, telling one of his somewhat risqué jokes to an enthralled audience, when the door was flung open, and a bunch of trouble filed in.

An old man sitting alone at a table was tipped out of his chair and onto the floor, and the group then gathered up several other chairs and sat down around the now vacant table.

'There's no need for that,' the barman called out, 'there are plenty of free tables.'

'We wanted that one,' one of the invading group replied, 'd'you want to make something of it?'

The barman, being a little more worldly wise, and unknown to most, had a shotgun beneath the bar. As he leaned down to get it, one of the men at the table drew a handgun and pointing it in the general direction of the bar, let off a shot.

Unfortunately, the bullet went wide and hit Cranford in the arm. The man at the table took aim again in Cranford's general direction, but by this time Cranford had reacted instinctively and drawn his own gun. His immediate reaction was to fire back at his assailant, hitting him squarely between the eyes - more by luck than judgment.

His assailant, with a look of shock on his face, fell backwards with the impact of the bullet and hit the floor with a resounding thud. Fortunately for Cranford, the other five men at the table were not carrying arms, but they all slowly rose from their seats, so he spun around on his bar stool and headed for the door with undignified haste.

Once outside, Cranford realised he was hopelessly outnumbered, and could expect little help from the other folks in the settlement, as very few of them seemed to carry guns. There was nothing for it, he would have to go on the run until things calmed down a little. But where to? The nearest little town was some sixty miles away, and then he heard raised voices and the muffled clatter of hooves on the dirt track between the little row of dwellings. If he kept on the track he would be overtaken in no time, so he took the first opportunity to turn off into the woods which surrounded the settlement, and headed uphill where the growth was denser and horses wouldn't be able to follow.

Cranford had been going for what seemed like hours, and still he could hear distant voices calling to one another, and the occasional gun shot. The higher he climbed, the rougher it got, huge blocks of stone had tumbled down the mountain until they hit the ones below and could go no further. At long last the ground levelled out a little, and he came upon what looked like an animal track, winding and twisting among the huge pine trees which covered the mountain. Being careful not to break a twig on the odd bush in case it betrayed his passage, Cranford followed the track, heading ever upwards as the light began to fail.

Exhausted, Cranford rested with his back against a huge pine, his legs gave way, and he slumped to the forest floor. His arm hurt, his head thumped, his throat was dry and felt as if it had been scrubbed with a wire bottle brush, and his chest ached. He had pushed his body well past the limits he usually imposed upon it, and it was telling him so. A while later, his agonising symptoms had eased somewhat, and he could hear without the pounding in his head. There were no distant voices calling, or gun shots, just the soft rustle of the pine tops as they swayed in the light breeze - he had outrun his pursuers.

Somehow Cranford got to his feet, although his body objected strongly, and staggered on up the path between the trees, not knowing quite why, but it seemed to be the right thing to do. Several times he tripped over unseen roots in the gloom, cursed, and went sprawling, and then just up ahead the trees thinned out and he could see the sky.

Before him was a stretch of open ground, and a log cabin with a light in the window, behind which the sheer rock face reared up to meet the darkening sky. He forced his body to cover the last few metres, and collapsed in a heap just as the door opened and a figure emerged.

Spitting out the dirt he had ingested when he fell, Cranford looked up to see an elderly man of stocky build, with long silver white hair looking down on him.

'You need some help,' the man said in a hard voice with a strange accent to it, 'come inside, and I will do what I can.'

Together they staggered into the cabin, the old man shutting the door behind them with a deft swing of his foot. It was snug and warm, and Cranford then realised just how cold it had been outside in the forest.

'You sit here,' said the old man, guiding Cranford to a wooden chair, 'I do things to your arm.'

He was in no shape to query or object to the offer, and so he just sat there, slumped down with his legs still shaking. A sharp knife removed the blood-soaked shirt, revealing the bullet hole in Cranford's upper arm. Fortunately, the bullet had passed straight through, just missing the bone, but leaving two neat holes which still seeped a little blood. Two small pads of material were daubed with a soft, cream-like substance and applied to the two holes in Cranford's arm, and bound in place. The old man put a small clot of Cranford's blood into a glass-like container which was then inserted into a black box he had taken from a shelf. After studying the top of the box for a few minutes, the old man opened a cupboard and took down several small containers, taking a measured amount from each and tipping them into a glass tumbler. Water was added, and the mixture went cloudy and then cleared. The old man nodded his approval of the mixture and put the tumbler to Cranford's lips.

'You drink this, it make you good again. You will sleep, and then you will be good.'

Cranford was past caring, and did as he was told. The liquid felt warm and sweet, and then his mouth tingled. Slowly the light in the cabin faded, flickered twice and went out.

When Cranford awoke, he had forgotten the trauma of the past day, although the memory of it was still clear in his mind when he looked. There was no pain in his arm and his legs felt normal again. He was lying on a soft bed which seemed to move gently beneath him so that his body kept flexing slightly.

'So you wake, that is good,' the old man said with what Cranford thought was an attempt at a smile, 'now you can stand up and tell me about you.'

Cranford related all that had happened to him over the past day - or was it two? - he wasn't sure. The old man listened intently, nodding every now and then to show he had understood the finer points of the traumatic event.

'You find it not easy to say my name, so call me Benie. What I call you?'

Cranford told him his name, and then asked, 'What is this place? It's miles from the settlement, and there's no road that I could see leading out. How do you get out?'

'I no need to get out. I live and work here, and have done so much time. You find my talking not like you? In time it will get better as I listen to you. We talk much. Now time to eat.'

Cranford wasn't sure if he liked this rather taciturn man. At least, he assumed it was a man, but not like any other he had met.

A meal of crusty bread, something like cheese, and a supply of fruit, most of which Cranford didn't recognise, went down well. This was followed by what he thought was beer of some kind - not like any beer he had ever drunk, but very palatable just the same. The meal was eaten in silence, and Cranford felt uncomfortable

'You said you work here, what do you do?' asked Cranford when the meal was over.

'Before I tell you, I must ask you some things about you.' Benie replied.

'OK,' said Cranford, 'ask away, I have nothing to hide, and nothing very exciting to talk about - except yesterday - that was certainly different!' Benie nodded, no emotion showing on his face.

At that moment a bell-like tone sounded, the old man got up, and with a slight limp, went over to the back wall of the cabin. When Cranford turned around to see where the old man had gone, there was no sign of him - just a blank wall. Cranford's feeling of unease increased to a point where he wanted to leave and take his chances out in the forest, but then common sense took over - there must be an explanation for the disappearance, he thought.

Just then there was a slight shake or shudder in the cabin, only just discernible, but there none the less. Cranford hurried to the door and went outside to see what had caused it, but the forest was just the same, the treetops softly swaying in the gentle breeze. 'God, that's weird,' he said to himself, as he went back in.

The old man was sitting in his seat as though nothing had happened - it was too much for Cranford. 'Where did you go, and what the hell was that shudder I felt just now?' he asked.

The old man slowly raised his hand as if to stop any further outbursts from Cranford, and then lowered it again. The silence seemed to drag on for ages, and then, after much thought, the old man spoke.

'Do you belong to any place, or other person?' asked Benie.

'Do you mean a wife or mate? No, I have none. Never got around to it, and I can live anywhere I choose. My life is a bit boring I suppose - didn't like city life so moved out to the settlement down below. That's OK, but not a lot happens there. Why do you ask?'

'I need to know about you, then I tell you about here,' replied Benie, a serious look on his weather-beaten face, 'This place not what you think. This place not just a cabin, it is much more. Do you want...' Benie paused for a moment, looking for the right word, '...a job of great interest and very good for many persons? It would be for long time, long, long time.'

'I might be interested, but I'd have to know a lot more of what it entails first. Sounds like a big commitment.' Cranford replied warily.

'Alright, I take a chance, as you say. I been here a long time. I would like to go to my own people now I old - but first I must find person to take my place - this I must do. I think you good person to work here, or I would send you away after making you good.' Benie paused, and went to refill the beer glasses. After drinking almost half his glass, Benie sat down again next to Cranford, and resumed the conversation.

'You look at me - what you see?'

Cranford was at a loss for words for a moment, and then he took a good long look at the man who had attended his injuries and made him welcome.

'Well, I see an old man, a very old man. But you are different to anyone I have ever seen before, come to think of it - don't know exactly what it is, but you are different.'

'Yes, I am different, as you say, but not in the way you think,' Benie replied, choosing his words carefully, 'I speak your language a little because I must. If other humans come here, they must think I one of them. Very few come up here, but I must be ready to speak with them if they do. The more I speak with you, the better I understand your language - you see, it is getting better.'

And then the penny dropped.

'You mean you aren't human?' Cranford gasped, 'you're not one of us! You are from - somewhere else?'

'Yes, I am. I look enough like your people to be accepted here, that is important for what I do. I bring no harm to your people, I just stay up here on the mountain and do my job - it harms no one and helps many.'

'OK, I can just about accept that, but what is your job exactly?' Cranford replied. 'All I see is an old man in a cabin up here on a mountain. You don't have any animals or even a vegetable patch - so how do you manage for food?'

'Everything I need is supplied, I not have to grow things, but I could if I want to,' Benie replied. 'What I do is important - I explain it to you.'

The old man got up and walked to the back of the cabin, beckoning Cranford to follow. He paused by the log wall, did something, and a section of the wall slid back silently, revealing another room beyond, cut into the cliff face.

'Come in,' Benie said to a hesitant Cranford. 'There is nothing here to harm you, but you will find it different to anything you have known before.'

The room was about twice the size of the log cabin, going back into the solid rock of the mountain. There was a deep, only just discernible hum, and the air had a faint electrical smell to it.

'What is this place?' asked an astonished Cranford, looking around in wonderment, 'you're right, I've never seen anything like this before.'

Around the walls, a series of gleaming cabinets stood like a row of soldiers, some with twinkling lights, others with knobs and switches, while two had glass screens which seemed to hover in and out of existence as Cranford moved about.

At the far end of the room stood two large transparent cylinders, side by side and mounted on plinths. They were big enough for several people to stand in, but at the moment were empty.

When Benie thought Cranford had seen enough of the complex, he said, 'We go back to the living in room, I will explain.'

With fresh glasses of beer, Benie sat down in the cabin opposite a bewildered looking Cranford, who was trying to make sense of what he had seen.

'I tell you about your world and other worlds,' began Benie, 'you stop me if you not understand. You see the Sun, and know your world goes around it in a circle?'

'Yes,' replied a dazed looking Cranford, 'everyone knows that, I suppose.

'You see stars in the sky at night - they are Suns also, and some of them have worlds going around them too. Many worlds have people living on them, and some are very advanced compared to your world. People need to travel from their worlds to other worlds sometimes, and I help them do that. You understand?'

'I hear what you say,' replied Cranford, 'but understanding it may take a little longer. Are you sure about these other worlds? I have never heard of them.'

'You will understand when I tell you some more,' said Benie patiently, taking a swig from his glass. 'You travel by coach and horse over big distance, and sometimes by a mechanical thing called a train. Horse can only go short distance between places, and then you have to get new horse to go on to where you want to go. It is the same in between worlds. The distance is very big, so there must be places to stop, and then go on. This is one of those places where travellers stop. I will show you how it works later, then you will understand. You want to ask something?'

Cranford sat in silence while he tried to make sense of what he had heard, and formulate a sensible question. The idea of people whizzing about in the sky was too much for him to comprehend, let alone understand.

At long last Cranford spoke, 'These people who go from world to world, are they like us? Do they look like us? Do they come to live on our world?'

Benie smiled, 'I am the only one to come to your world and live here, and I keep to this part of the mountain - I must not mix with your kind - it would be a big shock to them if they found out why I am here. The people who travel are much like us, I think all advanced intelligent life is much like us, but each world have their differences, like you and me.'

'But what if people came up here and found you, how could you explain all this? They may not like it and try to destroy it - you must know how odd some people are.'

'They would find a log cabin, an old man who was a bit strange, and go away. I would not explain anything to them. No one could destroy this place - even if they wanted to.'

'These other people, do they talk like you?' asked Cranford, unable to think of anything else to ask which made any sense.

'No, each world has its own language, some of which are very strange, even to me. But I have a thing called...' he paused again for a moment, 'called a translator. I do not know exactly how it works, but if someone speaks to it there is a little pause, and then you hear what they say in your language - very clever - only once did it not work for me.'

'OK, so what happens when people come here to stop over.' asked Cranford.

Benie was quiet for a moment, trying to simplify a very complicated answer into something a lay person could grasp.

'A person wants to travel to a distant world, but it so far away he must stop part way, not to actually rest, but for the machinery to make the distant connection. So, he comes here and waits for the correct portal to open, and then he is on his way to where he wants to go. Sometimes it is only minutes, and sometimes it may be as long as a day - depends which portals are busy. I enjoy these visits, I have met very interesting people here, and like their company very much - I think you will too - if you will work here.'

'Just suppose,' interjected Cranford, 'just suppose I decided not to work here, I might go out into my world and tell them about you and what you do here. That could cause a lot of trouble.'

Benie smiled, a little sadly, 'If that were so, I would have to wipe your memory clean of your visit here - you would wander about in the woods not knowing how you got there, but I think you would survive. I think you will stay, you are asking all the right questions, so you are interested - yes?'

'Must admit, I am,' replied Cranford, wishing he hadn't made the previous statement, 'it's just that I don't understand it all yet. It certainly sounds more interesting than what I have been doing up 'till now. You said you were very old, please explain that - there must have been many others like you here.'

'Not as many as you might suppose,' replied Benie, 'let me explain. I do not know quite how it works, but while I am in the cabin or the work room, or even outside in the little clearing, I do not age. Only when I am outside in the forest does normal ageing take place, and I do not go there very often.'

'So, you must be hundreds of years old,' said Cranford, trying to get his head around another astounding piece of data.

'Yes - many,' replied Benie with a sigh, 'but now I want to go back to my own people for the rest of my life, although all those I knew are long dead, but it just feels right, somehow.'

'Yes, I can understand that,' said Cranford, 'I'd feel the same way, I suppose. I felt comfortable with the people down in the settlement, although what it would feel like now, I don't know, those roughnecks certainly screwed things up a bit. Oh, screwed up - it means messed up, spoilt.' he added as an after thought.

Benie just smiled and nodded - he understood.

'Well, I think it is time for another meal,' said Benie. 'From what little I know of your people, you like animal meat - is that alright?'

'Yep - I sure could sink my teeth into a thick red steak,' Cranford replied, 'followed by apple pie and cream.' Benie just grinned. 'You go sit outside with another beer, and I will make the meal.'

Cranford sat in the old rocking chair as the sun began to sink, supped his beer and wondered what his friends down in the settlement would think of it all. The more he thought about the offer, the more it appealed to him.

The old man came out of the cabin bearing two plates, one of which he handed to Cranford. 'See if you like this,' he said, 'it may not be what you are used to, but I think you will like it.'

Cranford looked at his plateful to see if there was anything he could recognise, and failed. The meat was the right colour and fibrous, but there was no fat along the precision cut edges - it looked as if it had been cast in a mould. The vegetables were colourful if nothing else, but didn't quite resemble any he had ever seen before, but the first forkful of meat brought a smile to his face, and it continued as the vegetables were consumed.

'My God, that was good,' Cranford exclaimed, as he wiped his plate clean with a piece of crusty bread, 'and the gravy - sweet and sour together - that was brilliant. But I don't understand about the meat, there was no fat, and it looked moulded.'

'We don't eat meat from killed animals, it is grown in tanks and then pressed into the required shape. The vegetables are like those from my home world, although I do not know where they really come from - maybe they are synthetic too.' Benie said.

A fruit bowl was produced, but it only had one kind of fruit in it - and that looked like a peach, but was much bigger. The first bite put Cranford's mind at rest as the flavour exploded on his tongue, the juice ran down his chin, and he had to suppress a little giggle of delight.

'Thought you might like that,' said Benie, 'that too is from my home world.'

'I'm surprised you ever left it,' rejoined Cranford, as he wiped his chin clean.

The sun had almost set, lighting up the few clouds on the horizon in a blaze of yellow streaks while the forest below was almost black.

Just then a soft 'ping' broke their reverie, and Benie got to his feet and hurried to the cabin door. 'We will soon have a visitor,' he called out, 'you had better come in too.'

They went through the cabin and into the workroom beyond, the wall section closing behind them. One of the control units had a flashing light, and Benie went over to it, did something to the controls and stood back. The flashing light went out, and another one came on, a slight pause, and one of the transparent cylinders acquired a soft glow.

'Our visitor will soon be here,' Benie said in a formal tone. 'The flashing light was a request for transfer, the second light was my acceptance to say I am ready to receive, and the glow in the receiving chamber indicates that transmission is underway.'

A few seconds later the glowing cylinder went opaque - cleared - and a figure stood there, waiting for the cylinder to open. It was dressed in a smart dark grey uniform covering a thickset stocky body, a face chiselled out of granite and sleek combed back black hair. The cylinder opened, and the figure stepped out, pushed a small metal looking plate into the translator box, and the translator squawked several strange sounds. Benie reached for the box, and did something. With a slight bow of his head the stranger extended a hand, palm upwards. Benie stepped forward, dipped his head, and touched palms with the visitor.

'Well, that's the formalities over with,' came from the translator box, 'I thought you were alone here, who's your friend.'

Benie explained who Cranford was, adding that he might be taking over the operation in time, and was here to see if he thought the job was to his liking.

The visitor gave Cranford a stern look and the translator box said 'hmmm.' Neither of them was quite sure what that meant, so ignored it.

'Come on through,' said Benie to the visitor, who picked up the translator, and all three went into the cabin.

'Nice place you have here,' said the visitor, 'always enjoy coming here - you should see some of the places I pass through sometimes - you wouldn't want to go back.'

Cranford moved his chair a few steps back from the others, as he felt they knew each other quite well and probably had intimate things they wished to talk about. Benie did something to the translator box. The translator emitted strange sounds which Cranford found incoherent, so he just sat back and tried to make what sense he could of what had just happened.

Later, Benie disappeared for a few moments to return with refreshments, fruit and a sweet bread like lump, from which each broke off pieces when the mood took them.

A deep bell like tone sounded, and the visitor said, 'Oh well, time to go on I suppose, never get enough time here.' Or at least, that's what the translator box said.

The visitor stepped into the second cylinder which silently closed, Benie touched some symbols on a console, a light began flashing, stopped, another light came on, Benie touched a switch, the cylinder glowed, went cloudy, cleared and the glow went out.

'I know he looks stern, but that is just his looks - he is really very funny and a gentle person - known him for some time, but never stays very long. He is a controller for some of the big import export companies - always dashing about all over the place.'

'But how does the cylinder thing work?' asked Cranford, to whom the whole thing looked like a magic trick.

'It would take quite a long time to explain that,' said Benie, 'and I only know the basics. It is something to do with the warping of space and the time continuum - somehow two places can be in the same place at the same time for a very brief moment, and then they separate again - or something like that. If you decide to do this job, you will be able to access the scientific library on GN 43. I am sure they will be able to explain it to you. It would have interested me when I was a lot younger, but that was a long time ago.'

Benie steered Cranford from the workroom and out onto the open space outside the cabin. The sun had sunk, and the black velvet of the night sky was sprinkled with bright diamond-like twinkling stars, some with a hint of colour.

'You see those,' said Benie, pointing upwards, 'those are other suns, just like your own sun, but very, very far away - that is why they seem so small. Not all have worlds going around them. Of those that do, some have life on them - and some have intelligent life, like us. Some are very advanced, and have developed the ability to travel between the worlds. Because the distance is sometimes so great, it has to be done in stages - and that is where myself and others like me, make the connections between these worlds. Let us go back inside the cabin and sit down.'

Slowly, Cranford was beginning to make some sense of the seemly impossible - if his people could travel great distances on trains and boats, sometimes having to change to different ones, then why not... it was all a bit too much, but maybe...?

They sat there in silence for some minutes, Benie patiently waiting for his newfound friend to come to terms with that which he had to reconcile, those many years ago.

'I still don't understand why you think I would be good for this job,' Cranford said, after a while, 'you hardly know me, really.'

'One skill I have is to know people - somehow it matters little what race they come from - I just know,' Benie replied, hoping the explanation would not have to be expanded upon, 'and I think you would be ideal for the task.'

Cranford wasn't quite ready yet to commit himself to the proposed offer, so quickly changed the subject.

'That translator thing, how can that possibly work?' he asked.

'All of us who have to talk to others with a different language have our own translator, in which is a small plate with all the words of our language and a set of rules which place the words in the correct order. When another person wants to speak with me, they put their plate into the box, and using the two plates, the translator changes one language into the other.' Benie sat back, hoping his explanation would suffice.

'The correct order... Oh, I see,' Cranford exclaimed, 'We say 'I have a blue coat' while the French say 'I have a coat of blue.'

Benie looked a bit confused, 'I do not know about these French, who are they?'

'Oh, they are another race of people on this world who speak a different language to me,' Cranford replied, 'but how does the box do that?'

'That is something I do not need to know, so I have not been told. I can not explain it any more to you.'

'Alright, why didn't you use the translator when you talked to me?' asked Cranford.

'That is simple - I already speak some of your language, and you do not have a word plate to put into the box.' Benie replied, hoping to end the discussion on the subject.

Cranford thought for a moment - there were still too many things he didn't understand, and he needed to, in order to make a decision about the future.

'Another thing,' continued Cranford, 'where do you get the power to run all your equipment, I don't see a steam engine or a water wheel - or anything else, so where does it come from?'

'This is going to be difficult to explain to you, as you do not have the necessary words in your word bank - but I will try.' Benie resigned himself to trying to explain something of an advanced science, to someone who had little idea of what it was.

'*Basically*, what happens is that two hydrogen atoms, they are tiny particles of a gas, are forced to join together, and when they do so, they become another gas called helium - and a great deal of energy is released at the same time. This energy we turn into electricity - and that powers the equipment, and everything else.'

'I *think* I've got that,' Cranford replied, 'I've heard about electricity, but that comes from batteries.'

'Yes, but there are other ways of making it.' replied a somewhat frustrated Benie.

Before Cranford could come up with another awkward question,

Benie suggested they get some sleep, failing to tell him that the night might well be interrupted by the equipment in the cavern at the back of the cabin - there was no night or day for the transfer machine, or its varied travellers.

They had one more drink of Benie's beer, and then Cranford was assigned the bed he had rested on earlier, Benie explaining that the bed sensed strained muscles, and gently moved to sooth them; Benie then opened a cupboard on the wall and pulled down another sleeping pad, dimmed the lights, and lay down. Soon the gentle snoring of a tired Cranford was all that could be heard - except for the faint rustle of the fir trees outside.

Next morning, after a bit of thought, Cranford decided to take up Benie's offer, and become keeper of the Transfer Unit. It offered a chance of some excitement with all the different people going through the unit - and who knows where that may lead? Anyway, if he didn't like it, he could get someone else to do it, or just leave.

When he mentioned it to Benie at breakfast, he thought the old man looked relieved. After all, he had been there some considerable time, although he couldn't pin him down to exactly how long.

'First, we'll have to fit you up with a translator, and that means going to another world - I can't do it here. Anyway, I don't know exactly how it's done.' Benie said.

Cranford had his first pang of doubt - it was all right for others to go flitting about among the stars, but he didn't fancy it. Benie must have seen the look on his face.

'It is completely safe, we have been doing it for very long time, and no problems so far. You don't feel anything - just a slight disorientation for a split second - and you are somewhere else. Making the translator is simple, you just go into a light sleep for a while and all the words you use are somehow extracted from your mind and are put onto the speech plate we all have - you don't feel a thing.'

As breakfast drew to a close, it was agreed that Cranford would be put forward as the new keeper of the transfer unit. Benie went into the transfer room and must have contacted someone, as he came out with a big smile on his craggy face.

'It is all set up. Tomorrow, I will send you to the reception unit - they will make sure you want to become the new keeper, and then your speech plate will be made. You will then return here, and I will instruct you how to work the controls. When I think you have understood how everything works, an inspector will come and test you - and if you pass, and I am sure you will - you will be the new controller.' Benie positively beamed at Cranford.

He didn't sleep too well that night - dreams of whizzing through space and not knowing where he was heading left him in a cold sweat each time he woke up. When he eventually fell into a deep sleep, Benie woke him up. 'Time for breakfast,' he said cheerfully, 'and your great adventure begins.'

It didn't feel like it to Cranford, he felt sluggish, tired, his head had a dull ache, and the first few doubts had now crept into his mind. He felt better after one of Benie's breakfasts, and the doubts faded away.

Cranford stepped into the transparent cylinder which promptly closed, went misty, and opened again. He didn't know where he was, but it certainly wasn't the operations room behind the log cabin.

He was greeted by two very tall thin individuals, the skin on their faces looked as if it had been tightly stretched over a very knobbly skull, and then tightened some more. They seemed friendly enough, slightly bowing their heads as Cranford emerged from the transport cylinder, each extending a hand towards him, palm uppermost. Not knowing quite what to do, he placed his hand on theirs in turn.

'Please follow us,' one of the tall creatures said, 'we will talk with you.'

'How come you speak my language?' asked Cranford, somewhat surprised, 'I haven't made a language plate yet.'

'The operator of your unit sent us enough information to talk to you - it is necessary for the questions we must ask.'

They passed down a long corridor and into what Cranford thought was a lift of some kind, although it seemed to go sideways sometimes, and then they entered the interview room. It was sparse, just a table with a screen and something resembling a keyboard on it, several chairs, placed each side of the table, and a picture on the wall of which Cranford could make no sense of at all. One of the tall creatures waved Cranford towards a chair, so he obediently sat down facing the table, while the other two sat on the opposite side.

'Would you like to eat or drink?' the taller of the two asked in flat monotone.

'No thanks, I did before I left the transfer unit.' replied Cranford, not wishing to sample some alien food which might revolt him, thereby insulting his hosts by refusing it. They both nodded in acknowledgment.

The questions began, and Cranford was surprised at their grasp of his language. Some questions seemed pointless to him, while others probed deeply into his psychological being. He didn't mind, as he had nothing to hide. All the while, the slightly shorter of the two tapped away at the keypad before him, nodding every now and again, but whether it was in agreement with his answers or not, Cranford had no way of knowing. After what seemed like hours to Cranford, his hosts sat back in their chairs as one, nodded their heads, and did what Cranford took to be a smile.

'We thank you for your answers, your reasons for being an operator meet our requirements. We will now make a speaking plate for you to take back.'

Cranford got up from his chair, as did the other two, and then back into the lift thing. Up, sideways, down, and into another room. A long-padded bench, with an array of odd looking equipment at its head, was all there was to be seen. The taller thin man gestured towards the bench, and Cranford climbed onto it, feeling a little uneasy as he did so - it was too late to back out now, so he just lay down and hoped for the best.

'You will sleep for some time, and then you may return to your unit.' The taller of the two said, again with what Cranford thought was a smile.

The tall one did something to the equipment behind Cranford's head, the room faded from view, and he slipped into a light sleep. He was dreaming, but like no dream he had ever had before. He was talking very fast, to someone or something, but it was so fast he couldn't understand what he was saying.

Eventually, the room came back into view, and only one of the tall people was present, gently helping Cranford to his feet.

'God, I feel stiff,' was all he could say.

'You will soon be recovered, and we have your translator box ready for you to take back. The operator of your unit will teach you how to work the equipment, and you will be assessed by one of us to see if you are....' he paused, trying to find the right word, '...competent to do so.'

Once more into the lift thing - by the time they had reached the transfer room, Cranford was feeling decidedly dizzy, and was glad to be on his way home.

The cylinder closed around him, went misty, opened, and there was Benie, all smiles.

'How long have I been gone?' was Cranford's first question.

'About three of my days, but I don't know how much of your time has gone - this transfer thing can mess time about, so I've been told. Anyway, it's good to have you back. Are you hungry?'

'I could eat a bloody horse,' replied Cranford, 'although I don't suppose you've got one.' Benie had that puzzled look on his face for a second, and then laughed.

'That was great,' said Cranford, after the meal, 'you sure know how to make someone feel welcome. Oh, and that brings me to something else. What about food, when you're gone? How will they know what to send me?'

'Do you like what you have been eating since you have been here? If so, just leave things as they are and your food will be sent. If you wish to change it, let me know.'

'I think I'll stick to your food - it's great.' replied Cranford, cramming in another chunk of the flavoursome bread like thing, which was all that was left on the table.

And then began many days of hard training, at the end of which Cranford was surprised at his own competence, and Benie was grinning from ear to ear.

Two days later, and the assessor arrived; Cranford passed the examination with flying colours, as his fingers flew over the controls like he had been doing it all his life.

A couple of weeks later, and Benie announced that he was ready to return to his people. Knowing full well that any of his friends and relations were long gone, he still felt he would like to pass the rest of his days among his own kind, and Cranford agreed - he would do the same, if he were Benie.

It wasn't until the actual parting was about to take place, that they both realised the bond which had grown between them. There were tears in both pairs of eyes as Benie stepped into the transporter and the cylinder closed - a split second later and the cylinder opened - empty.

It was many weeks later before the loneliness wore off, helped by a very busy time in the transporter room.

Cranford settled into his new job with a degree of enthusiasm he hadn't experienced for a very long time. Some of his visitors were a bit taciturn, saying very little, but most seemed glad to have someone to talk to while they waited for the transfer machine to make the necessary connections to send them on their way.

Slowly, over the years, he made friends with some of the more regular visitors as his predecessor, Benie, had done.

Looking out of the window one day, Cranford noticed a man dressed in unusual attire and with a gun in the crook of his arm looking at the cabin. Curious as to how anyone had found his retreat, he went out to greet the visitor.

'Hi there, are you lost?' was his opening gambit.

'Not exactly,' came the reply from a middle-aged man dressed in buckskin, with a hat sporting a racoon tail and a back-pack, 'I left the little township down below and headed up the mountain after someone said no one ever goes there - thought it might be interesting to find out why. Must say, it's one hell of a struggle to get up here - not surprised no one does. So, what do you do here?'

'Not much, I just like my own company,' replied Cranford, being very careful what he said, 'I don't mind the solitude - gives me plenty of time to think,' he added as an afterthought.

'Must say, you get one hell of a view from up here,' the stranger said, looking out over the endless mountains and valleys, 'wouldn't mind a little place like this myself.'

The silence seemed to drag on for ages, Cranford dreading the next awkward question his visitor might ask.

'Suppose you get your supplies dropped in by helicopter,' the stranger said at last.

Cranford, not knowing the term, stopped himself just in time from asking what a helicopter was, and said, 'something like that. Would you like a home-made beer? Just made a new brew.'

'Sure would.' the stranger replied, sitting himself down in Cranford's old rocking chair.

Cranford hurried into the cabin, wondering how he could get the stranger off his property before he was asked questions that he had no answers for.

Two beers later, and the stranger said, 'God, this is awesome stuff, can't get this in any bar I've ever been in, where did you learn to make it?'

'Old family recipe,' Cranford replied. 'What news of the world outside?' he asked, changing the subject.

'Don't you have a radio or television?' the stranger asked, surprised.

'Mine's broken, and I can't seem to fix it.' replied Cranford, thinking on his feet.

'I've got a small one in my back-pack,' the stranger answered, 'don't use it much. You can have it in exchange for another beer. It's one of these new windup ones. You just wind the handle up for a few minutes, and it will work for ages. No need for batteries, you see. Just noticed, you don't seem to have any aircraft around here, not even any con trails from the high-flying ones - must be off the main routes, I suppose.'

'Yep, I guess that's it,' said Cranford, dreading the next awkward question or comment.

They chatted on for a while, when the stranger said, 'Guess I'd better be going, don't want to get caught up here in the dark - it was difficult enough in daylight, thanks for the beer. If I'm ever up this way again, I'll drop in and see you.'

With that the stranger got to his feet, shook hands, and somewhat unsteadily headed off in the direction he had come. Cranford, although he enjoyed the company of his own kind after so long, heaved a sigh of relief as the tension of being on guard against awkward questions or a signal from the transfer unit, was beginning to get to him.

The windup radio intrigued him - he gave the handle several winds, not knowing quite what to expect, pressed the on switch, and then turned the tuning dial. He nearly dropped the radio as music blared out at him. Cranford knew about the wired telegraph, and on one occasion had used it - so this must be some means of sending messages and music without wires. He then began to wonder just how long he had been up on the mountain, and what other inventions had come about since he had forsaken civilisation. The stranger had mentioned aircraft, without saying what they were - and Cranford didn't dare ask. Craft was something he could understand, so aircraft must be something which travelled through the air - it still didn't make much sense.

Later, when one of his friends stopped over while the transfer unit hunted about for the right connection, he asked about the mysterious aircraft the stranger had mentioned, and learned that some places had machines which flew like a bird and transported people about around their world, but there were better ways of travelling.

Listening avidly to his radio, and querying anything he didn't understand with the travellers passing through the transfer unit, Cranford was able to build up a picture of what was happening on Earth. He had no idea of how much 'real' time had passed on Earth since he had taken on the job at the transfer unit, and wondered how things could advance so quickly compared to the life he had known before.

Glorious summers and winter snows came and went, and Cranford was growing more and more uneasy about the state of his home world. It would seem that there now existed three main power groups, each armed to the teeth and fighting a trade war among themselves - as the use of the new terror weapons would erase humankind from the face of the Earth, his concern mounted.

The radio kept him up to date with events, that's if they could be believed. So far as Cranford was concerned, man's insanity had taken a turn for the worst, and he just couldn't understand why.

He discussed his concerns with some of his travelling friends, but generally they just accepted it as being normal for some races, although they had not personally encountered such madness themselves. From what Cranford could glean from his visitors, the rest of the Universe seemed to have got it right - no wars - even trading wars - and everyone reasonably happy.

Cranford was kept busier than usual for some time, sending his travellers on their way, so when he next tuned in his radio, the news was not good. Two of the power blocks accused each other of dumping nuclear waste on each other's territories, both finding it very hard to prove, while three high level assassinations had taken place, and no one could find out who was responsible. Sabre rattling seemed to be the order of the day, each power block accusing the other two of perpetrating the felonious events.

One day, Cranford saw something new - white vapour trails very high up in the sky. To his mind this could only mean one of two things - surveillance aircraft keeping an eye on the opposition, or worse still, armed missiles going into orbit ready to strike.

Frequent news bulletins spoke of the increasing tension between the great powers, and what each would do to the other if things turned nastier than usual.

He had spoken of his concerns to some of his visitors to see if anyone would intervene if requested, but the general answer was that each world had to sort its own problems out - only if one world was threatened by another, would the Federation intervene.

Each time Cranford tuned in his radio, it seemed that the voice pitch had gone up a notch, tinged with an ever-increasing level of panic. He wondered why none of his 'friends' had shown any concern for his wellbeing, should the worst come to the worst - and then remembered that the transfer unit somehow existed in its own space/time continuum - he at least was safe. Was he to be the only human being left in existence, if some idiot pressed the button? Cranford found himself trembling at the thought - this was raw fear, the like of which he had not experienced before.

For a while, Cranford's mind had been taken off the apparent impending doom, as the transfer unit hit a particular busy phase. He had seen the last visitor off to his destination, and was sitting outside the cabin enjoying a beer and the slowly sinking sun, marvelling at its beauty, when he switched on his radio.

The voice did its best to remain steady and calm, but the raw panic came through just the same. 'You are advised to seek shelter in your bunkers - I repeat, go to your bunkers now. Last minute negotiations have broken down - God help us all.' The radio crackled and hissed several times before going dead. Cranford's trembling hand turned the tuning dial, picking up a foreign station, but that soon turned to hiss and crackle too. So, was this it - mankind about to pull the plug on itself?

Cranford went back into the cabin and pulled the curtains, something he had never done before. A few minutes later, and the first of several brilliant flashes of intense light lit up the inside of the cabin, and Tumblerock Mountain trembled.

THE END

If you have enjoyed this book, please consider leaving a review on Amazon. It would mean a lot to us.

Other books by David Reynolds-Moreton

The Seed Garden
Extreme Difference
Exchange Rate
The Martian Enigma
The Single Twin
Transplant
Greenways
The Tribe
The Sweepers
Of wood, Metal, and Glass
Enslavement
Flight of the Tristan
Divergence
Life Force
Anthology of Possibilities
Light Quest
Intervention
The Power Seeds
Inheritance
Zuki
Fully Guaranteed

Audio Books
Transplant | Greenways | The Tribe | The Seed Garden

Scan the QR code below to discover these titles online

About the Author

"Back in 1998 I was commenting to a friend that I didn't go much on so called modern Science Fiction. It didn't seem as good or as interesting as the adventures stories written by the old masters of sci-fi – Clarke, Russell, Pohl, Asimov, Heinlein etc. His reaction was 'well, write your own then' – As I already had an idea at the back of my mind, I did. After printing up ten copies and binding them (hardback) they were passed around among like minded friends – and then came the request for more of the same! Again and again. Only one problem – I was spending too much time printing and binding and not writing, which I enjoy. Getting into 'print' is difficult – if not impossible – so I chose the 'eBook' route. I would recommend it to anyone who likes writing, and has a story to tell."

David (aka D.B) Reynolds-Moreton is a retired research and development engineer who lives in Devon, England with his wife. You can read a short biography of his life and adventures in science at :

www.sci-fi-cafe.com/david-reynolds-moreton

www.ingramcontent.com/pod-product-compliance
Lightning Source LLC
Chambersburg PA
CBHW030807190726
48285CB00003B/1056